Froth, Fiction, and Felony

A Piper Page Cozy Mystery

Lucy Penbrook

Froth, Fiction, and Feloncy

Lucy Penbrook
2222 W Harry St
Wichita KS 67226
lucy@lucypenbrook.com

Cover design by Lyssa @ BookedForeverShop
Edited by Stacey Goitia

First Edition: September 2025

Published by Lucy Penbrook Press

ISBN: 9798992382211

Printed in the United States of America

For more information about the author and upcoming books, visit www.lucypenbrook.com

Contents

Prologue

♥

The pre-dawn light barely made a dent in the darkness as I walked down the narrow staircase from my loft above Books and Brew. Jazz, my tuxedo cat, was close at my heels, nearly tripping me as I headed down. Today was the kickoff of the Maplebrook Pages and Prose Festival. I'd been looking forward to it for months, and it was a huge undertaking for my little store. I needed the event to be a massive hit; my finances were not what I'd hoped over the last few months, and the weeklong literary event could be the very thing I needed to help get me back into the black.

"It's going to be a long day, buddy," I whispered to Jazz, who meowed softly in response as if in agreement. He looked back at me, leading me further down the stairs with a very purposeful trot. We were on Jazz's food schedule now, and I was late getting his morning treats.

Stepping into the familiar embrace of the bookstore, I flicked on the lights, chasing away the shadows and revealing the cozy chaos of books and comfy chairs awaiting the day's customers. The festival had been months in the planning, and now, with everything in place, excitement thrummed through me, mingled with a thread of nervous energy. I really couldn't afford for anything to go wrong.

As I made my way to the front of the store to prepare for the day, I noticed a piece of paper just under the front door. "What is it?" I mused aloud, bending to pick it up with Jazz circling my feet. He nosed at the envelope, trying to chew on the corner before I could look inside.

I pulled it back from and unfolded it. Inside, I found a message written in hurried penmanship, its contents sending a shiver down my spine. "*Piper, the truth about Maplebrook is not what it seems. Trust no one.*" There was no signature, just a cryptic warning.

I stared at the note and at Jazz, who looked back with his inscrutable, green eyes. "Seems we've got a mystery on our hands," I said, half to him, half to myself.

Jazz responded with a purr, as if to say, "What are we waiting for?"

Chapter One

♥

I tried to shake off the uneasiness I felt after reading the mysterious note – why wasn't I supposed to trust anyone, and what was with the truth about Maplebrook not being what it seemed? I stuffed it in my apron pocket and started getting ready for the busy day ahead. I thought about calling my best friend Zoe and telling her about the note, but I already felt overwhelmed with all I had to do. Jazz seemed to sense the shift in my mood, his head cocked to one side as if questioning my sudden quietness.

"Big day, Jazz," I said, attempting to sound more upbeat than I felt. "The entire town will be here for the Pages and Prose Festival. And guess who's the star of the show?" I paused, eyeing him. "No, not you, you furry narcissist. Professor Emerson! Though I bet if you show everyone your fluffy belly, you will get plenty of attention."

Jazz meowed, unimpressed by my attempt to deflect my unease with humor. He jumped down from his perch to rub against my leg. I wanted to think it was a gesture of solidarity, but I knew it was likely just a reminder of his breakfast time. I filled his bowl with his favorite food (a rabbit a cranberry pâté, perfect for my discerning fuzzball), and freshened his water. He gobbled it up, wasting absolutely zero time.

Books and Brew, my beloved bookstore and coffee shop, was nestled within an old limestone house, and today, it was playing a key role in hosting the festival's inaugural event: a lecture by the esteemed Professor Emerson. It was an honor, a responsibility, and now, with the discovery of the note, apparently a mystery. What it had to do with me, I didn't know.

I took over Books and Brew just last year after my grandma Eleanor passed away and left the store to me. Growing up in Maplebrook, I went to the local college and got a degree in Literature, where my love for mysteries and detective stories really took off. After graduation, I spent a few years working at the city library in Kansas City, learning all there was to know about books and people. But after my grandma's death, I came back to run Books and Brew. I just hope I didn't let her down.

Shaking off my anxiety, I focused on the task at hand, preparing Books and Brew for its moment in the spotlight. "Let's get to it," I said, more to myself than to Jazz, who had already returned to his window spot, the unofficial overseer of our little corner of Maplebrook. The note would have to wait; the festival—and my curious cat—demanded my attention.

I moved on to one of the morning rituals which brought me as much joy as it did to my customers. The glass bakery displays by the counter, previously empty, awaited their daily transformation into a showcase of local delights. "Time to make the café smell irresistible, Jazz," I remarked, knowing full well my feline companion was far more interested in the warm sunbeam than the day's tasks.

One by one, I arranged the pastries, each a work of art from The Sugar Whisk. I took pride in sourcing locally, supporting other small businesses which, like Books and Brew, had become a staple in our community. The Hearth's offerings were always a hit with our patrons, from flaky croissants which melted in your mouth to rich, chocolatey brownies which had a habit of disappearing almost as soon as I could set them out. "Looks good enough to eat, doesn't it?" I mused aloud, though Jazz seemed unfazed, his attention momentarily caught by a bird outside.

One benefit of owning the bookstore and café was I could sample the goodies anytime I wanted. Quality control, after all. I pulled a slice of banana nut bread from the case and took a bite. Evie had outdone herself again. The subtle bitterness of the walnuts complemented the sweetness of the bananas, and the vanilla and cinnamon added just the right warmth and depth. A coconut drizzle topped the bread and made me want to eat the entire loaf, but then my skinny jeans just would not button later.

As I finished setting up, my thoughts drifted to the lecture we were hosting tonight. "Professor Emerson is going to reveal some of Maplebrook's hidden histories right here, Jazz. Can you believe it?" I whispered, more to myself, feeling a mix of excitement and responsibility. "It's such a big deal for Books and Brew."

I paused and looked around the room which would soon fill with eager listeners, feeling my heart swell with a sense of purpose. I'd worked hard over the last five years, growing my little shop. There had been some rough patches, especially getting things off the ground. It had taken every bit of blood, sweat, and tears I had—not to mention money — to make it something special, but it had finally grown into just the place I wanted it to be.

"Let's hope everything goes smoothly," I continued, half-expecting Jazz to offer a reassurance. I hadn't told my friends or co-workers, but with the downturn in the economy, we'd been struggling a little financially. The increased sales the festival would bring us could be huge, and I was really relying on the income.

Jazz merely stretched, utterly unconcerned with the complexities of hosting a lecture. "At least one of us isn't worried," I chuckled, allowing myself a moment of envy for his simple contentment.

I moved towards the heart of our coffee operation. The coffee shop area, with its vintage espresso machine and rose quartz tabletops, was one of my favorite areas in the shop. Chairs upholstered in different shades of pink and delicate China cups contrasted beautifully with the dark, aromatic coffee we served. It was like stepping into a different era, one where time slowed down just enough for you to savor the moment.

Just as I was about to flip the switch and start the brew, the door chimed. Lottie Jenkins breezed in in her usual, unmissable fashion. With her bright smile, energy which could power the entire café, and grey hair styled in a trendy cut which matched her vivacious personality, Lottie wasn't just my co-worker, she was a mentor and a great friend. I couldn't run my place without her.

"Morning, Piper! Have the bookshelves started whispering their secrets yet, or do they wait for the caffeine to kick in?" Lottie's vibrant attire was a stark contrast to the calm hues of dawn filtering through the windows. Her scarf today was a riot of colors, as if challenging the pink dominance of Books and Brew.

I couldn't help but laugh, turning to her with a smile. "They're tight-lipped this morning. I think they're waiting for your magic touch."

Lottie winked, setting down her bag with a flourish. "Let's not keep them in suspense too long. The world needs its coffee, and I need my daily dose of drama from the pages of the unread." She approached the counter, glancing at the pastry display. "Looks like Evie outdid herself again. How do you make these pastries look even more delicious? Is there some kind of secret bookish spell involved?"

"Strategic placement and good lighting. It also helps to sample the merchandise," I replied, playing along. "But if you find a spell book, let me know. We could use it for the lecture tonight."

"Ah, yes. Do you think we'll survive the influx of history buffs and mystery seekers?" Lottie teased, her eyes twinkling as she began her morning routine of prepping the café.

"Only if we keep the coffee flowing and the mysteries contained to the pages of our books," I countered, finally starting the espresso machine. I made myself a strong one and handed Lottie her favorite blend of Morning Glory Medium Roast; it was going to be a long day, and we needed a caffeine jolt to get through it.

Just as the first cups of coffee found their hands into the eager grips of our morning customers and the hum of Books and Brew settled into a comfortable rhythm, the door chimed again. This time, Zoe Palmer walked in.

Zoe was my very best friend, a local artist and the owner of Palette Whispers. Her personality was what I'd describe as eclectic, as she often wore her hair in changing colors. Today it was a bold shade of teal.

"Morning, gals!" Zoe called out. She held a collection of colorful flyers and a folder bulging with what I assumed were her latest inspirations.

Lottie shot me a knowing glance before turning to Zoe. "And what grand scheme do you have for us today? Something that involves turning Books and Brew into an art installation?"

"Not quite, but you're on the right track," Zoe replied with a laugh, laying her materials on the counter. She pulled out several prints, each more captivating than the last, showcasing the work of local artists. "I was thinking, with the lecture happening tonight, why not add an extra layer of local flavor? We could display some artwork to support our talented community."

The idea immediately resonated with me. "I love it," I said, genuinely excited. "It's the perfect way to highlight our local artists."

Zoe beamed, pleased with the reception. "I've already talked to a few. They love the idea and will lend us their pieces for the evening. It could be a mini exhibition, a conversation starter, and who knows? It might even inspire Professor Emerson's storytelling."

I nodded, imagining the walls of Books and Brew adorned with local art, each piece adding depth and context to the lecture. "It'll be a celebration of Maplebrook's culture and creativity. And it's just what makes Books and Brew special."

Jazz chose the moment to glide through the room. He rubbed against Zoe's leg, earning a gentle scratch behind the ears. He purred and flopped down, rolling over with no regard for personal space. When he wanted belly rubs, he wanted them now.

"Even Jazz approves. We're definitely onto something." Zoe laughed, bending to rub his belly and whisper something in his ear, as if he was in on the plan, too. She chuckled as Jazz sauntered off, his mission apparently completed. "You know, Piper, if we ever run out of ideas, we should just consult Jazz. He seems to have a knack for this."

I chuckled, glancing at the spot by the window where Jazz had resumed his watchful vigil. "He's got an eye for art—or at least, for people who appreciate it."

Lottie returned just then, her arms full of a new shipment of books. "Speaking of eyes for art, I heard we're turning Books and Brew into Maplebrook's newest gallery. Do I need to practice my art critic lingo?"

"Only if you can do it without scaring the customers," I teased. "We're aiming for 'inviting,' not 'intimidating'."

Lottie set down the books with a dramatic flourish. "Darling, I am nothing if not the epitome of inviting. Besides, with Piper's memory, we'll have the backstory of every piece and artist ready to share. It'll be like a live audio guide, but with more charm and less monotone."

Zoe grinned. "Piper, your brain is basically the secret weapon of Books and Brew. Is there anything you don't remember?"

I felt a flush of pride mixed with a hint of sheepishness. "I haven't forgotten to water Jazz's catnip plant yet, so there's that."

"See? Invaluable," Lottie quipped. "Now, if only your memory could solve the mystery of who keeps eating the last piece of cake in the breakroom."

"Ah, but maybe it can," Zoe winked. "Or better yet, maybe it'll solve a genuine mystery for us one of these days."

"Speaking of mysteries," I said, feeling the weight of the anonymous note in my pocket as if it were made of lead. I guided her away from the cheerful bustle of the store to a quiet corner. Her curiosity was palpable as I handed her the folded paper, my hands slightly trembling.

Zoe unfolded it and skimmed, her expression turning serious. "Piper, this could be serious. Shouldn't we go to the police?"

I bit my lip, considering. "I don't know. Part of me wonders if it's just some kind of elaborate prank."

Zoe looked at me, skeptical. "This doesn't feel like someone's idea of a joke, Piper. It feels...deliberate. But if you think it's best to wait, I trust your judgment. Just promise me we'll keep an eye out for anything unusual, okay?"

I nodded, tucking the note back into my pocket. "I promise to be extra vigilant. With the festival and everything, Books and Brew will be bustling. Perfect for some observational sleuthing."

"And who knows, tonight's lecture might just shed some light on our little enigma," Zoe said, being optimistic. "Maplebrook's history is about to get a lot more interesting."

My nerves, however, remained on edge. "I just hope it's the right kind of interesting. Something about this feels bigger than we're ready for."

"Did I hear 'mystery note' being bandied about?" Lottie's voice cut through before Zoe could reassure me further. "And here I was, thinking today was just about books and history."

At that moment, a customer, drawn by Lottie's exclamation, edged closer, curiosity piqued. Lottie turned to her with a theatrical sigh. "Sorry, dear, autographs from the town's top sleuths will have to wait until after the festival. We're in the middle of plotting—er, planning the day."

I couldn't help but smile. Lottie's humor was a welcome reprieve. "We're discussing whether to bring in the calvary over an anonymous tip," I explained, glancing between my two friends.

Lottie's eyes sparkled with mischief. "How deliciously noir. We're like a trio of detectives in a pulp fiction novel. Piper, the keen-eyed leader; Zoe, the artistic soul with a knack for code-breaking; and me, the wise-cracking sidekick with a heart of gold."

Zoe laughed, the tension in the air lightening. "Lottie, only you could turn our predicament into a casting call for a detective agency. But Piper's right, we need to be careful. Until we know more, let's keep this to ourselves."

"Agreed," I said. "Tonight, we focus on the lecture and the festival. But we keep our ears open. Whoever left this note wanted it to be found, and I have a feeling it is only the beginning."

Lottie nodded, her usual joviality a bit tempered. "Let's make sure it's a beginning we can handle. Together, there's nothing we can't solve."

Chapter Two

♥

Lottie and I were arranging a selection of light snacks in the cafe area of Books and Brew, the delicate clink of dishes punctuating our preparations for the evening's lecture. "These mini quiches will disappear faster than a good mystery novel on a rainy day," Lottie said, placing the last of the quiches on a tiered stand.

The Sugar Whisk, a gem in our small town, had provided the quiches, along with an assortment of delectable pastries. Evie Bennett, the bakery's owner, came by to add her expertise to the setup. "Just save a couple of those for me," Evie joked, her warm smile lighting up the room.

"You'll have to fight me for them." I gave her a friendly nudge. If I was being honest, I'd already snuck one when no one was looking. Okay, two, but who was counting?

"Evie, Books and Brew is lucky to have you as part of our festival kickoff," I said, admiring the arrangement.

She smiled warmly. "It's my pleasure. Anything to support the festival and your lovely gathering."

With the quiches set and the coffee brewing, I turned to the rest of the group. "Aside from tonight's lecture, what other festival events are you all looking forward to? I've got a pretty packed schedule, but

I'm especially excited about the writer's workshop and the poetry slam we're hosting later this week."

Zoe's eyes lit up. "Oh, I'm *definitely* attending the poetry slam. And don't forget the children's story hour, Piper. I've heard rumors of a certain someone dressing up as their favorite literary character."

Lottie laughed, nudging Zoe playfully. "No chance I'd miss seeing you in costume, Zoe. I'm also looking forward to the local author's panel. Did you hear that Julia Hart is going to be here?" Lottie fanned herself. "I cannot wait to get my favorite author's autograph!"

Evie nodded in agreement. "Don't forget the culinary literature evening. It's right up my alley, pairing delicious treats with passages from beloved books. I've been brainstorming new recipes all week."

It sounds like we're all in for a busy, but incredibly rewarding week," I said, feeling hopeful the festival was going to be just what my store needed for a surge in sales.

As we shared a collective moment of appreciation for the upcoming festivities, the bell above Books and Brew's door chimed and Miranda Clarke waltzed in. Miranda was the town's historian. She was always dressed to the nines, and tonight was no exception. She rocked a tailored emerald-green suit with a silk blouse that had the cutest lace trim. It was topped off with a string of pearls and matching emerald earrings that screamed elegance.

"Good evening, Piper," she greeted, her voice cool but courteous. "I see Books and Brew is embracing the festival spirit wholeheartedly."

"We are," I replied, striving for a balance between warmth and formality. "It's a great opportunity to delve into Maplebrook's past and bring the community together."

Miranda's gaze sharpened as she pointed a perfectly manicured nail at me. "That's precisely my concern. The content of Professor Emerson's lecture tonight—his theories could stir up unnecessary controversy."

Before I could respond, Lottie walked in with a tray of mini quiches in hand. "But a little controversy makes for good conversation, doesn't it? Like how I insist that pineapple really *does* belong on pizza."

The attempt to lighten the mood drew a brief, reluctant smile from Miranda. "I appreciate the attempt at humor, but this is serious. Piper, surely you understand the potential consequences of allowing such...divisive topics to be aired so publicly."

"Lottie has a point, though," I said, hoping to bridge our perspectives. "Books and Brew is more than a bookstore; it's a place for open conversation. We trust our community to engage with ideas thoughtfully."

Miranda sighed, the lines of her face softening slightly. "Conversation is one thing, but rewriting history is quite another. Not all revelations are beneficial."

As she turned to leave, Lottie leaned in toward me.. "If history was written in stone, we wouldn't need historians, would we?" she whispered, loud enough for Miranda to hear.

Miranda paused, offering no comeback, her departure leaving a silence which spoke volumes. Lottie turned to me, her expression a mix of concern. "Don't worry, Piper. Books and Brew has always been about opening minds, not closing them. Tonight will be no different."

After Miranda's exit, the tension she'd brought with her seemed to dissipate. Lottie placed the tray of mini quiches down with a decisive clatter and turned to me with a twinkle in her eye.

"That was as fun as a surprise quiz on a Monday morning. Now, where were we before our brief history lesson?"

Lottie's humor was much needed after the exchange with Miranda. The last thing I needed tonight was any additional stress. Zoe, having overheard the tail end of our exchange from where she was adjusting the placement of a painting, chimed in with a grin. "Plotting to overthrow the strictures of historical accuracy, are we? Count me in."

I couldn't help but laugh, feeling the weight of the day lighten. "All in a day's work at Books and Brew. Next, we'll be accused of harboring a secret society dedicated to the unconventional reading of history."

Lottie leaned closer. "Who says we aren't?" she whispered conspiratorially. "I've always fancied the idea of a cloak and a secret handshake."

Zoe joined us at the counter, her eyes shining with excitement. "In all seriousness, though, tonight is going to be incredible. Emerson's lecture, the art, these delicious quiches—how could it be anything but?"

The energy between us was infectious. "We're expecting a packed house. I hope I have enough tables and chairs ready. And enough quiches," I added, thinking of the ones I'd eaten already. "Maplebrook has seen nothing like it in years."

As the clock ticked closer to the start of the event, we moved through our final preparations, the excitement palpable. "Alright, team," I said, looking around at the space we'd transformed together. "Let's show Maplebrook what Books and Brew is all about. Here's to a night of history, mystery, and maybe a little bit of mischief."

Lottie raised an imaginary glass. "To Books and Brew. May our minds be opened, our hearts full, and our quiches plentiful."

"To Books and Brew," I cheered.

An hour later, the buzz of excitement was palpable as the cafe area of Books and Brew transformed into a vibrant hub of intellectual curiosity and community spirit. Every table was filled, with more guests standing along the walls, their eager faces illuminated by the soft, inviting glow of string lights we had put up for the occasion. Fifty people, maybe more, had gathered in our cozy little nook, all buzzing with anticipation for Professor Emerson's lecture.

"I've never seen Books and Brew this packed," Zoe remarked, weaving her way through the crowd to join me behind the makeshift bar we'd set up for refreshments. "It feels like the whole town turned out."

I couldn't help but smile, pride swelling in my chest. "It's not every day we uncover the hidden chapters of our town's history," I replied, pouring two cups of coffee before handing one over to her. "I just hope everyone finds the evening as enlightening as they're expecting."

Lottie was making rounds and ensuring everyone felt welcome and comfortable. She paused near us, her eyes gleaming with excitement. "If the buzz is anything to go by, we're in for quite the night. Piper—your knack for bringing people together is nothing short of magical."

Lottie's words were still hanging in the air when Sophie Turner, Maplebrook's most diligent and inquisitive journalist, made her way through the packed cafe. Known for her sharp wit and even sharper pen, Sophie had a knack for capturing the essence of Maplebrook's happenings in her articles. She also had a knack for twisting words to get stories when there wasn't one.

"Piper, a moment for the press?" Sophie called out, her voice cutting through the buzz of conversations with practiced ease. Her hair was styled into the cutest, blonde pixie cut, and she was always dressed in the latest fashions. Perfectly manicured nails waved in the air as she beckoned me over to her.

Inwardly, I rolled my eyes. I always felt frumpy next to Sophie, and I could tell she disapproved of my appearance as she took in my knee-high brown leather boots, pink, puffy-sleeved sweater, and simple gold-hooped earrings. But really – why would I need to dress up to shelve books and pour coffee? "Sophie, always on the hunt for the next big headline," I greeted her, my tone light but wary.

Sophie's eyes twinkled with excitement—or perhaps it was the scent of a story in the air. "You've outdone yourself. Books and Brew is just the talk of the town, and with the Pages and Prose Festival kicking off tonight, everyone's eager to know what you have in store."

"We aim to please—and to provoke thought," I replied, conscious of the many ears tuned to our exchange. "Tonight's lecture by Professor Emerson is just the beginning. We've got a week filled with events that we hope will bring our community even closer."

Sophie scribbled notes, her eyes not leaving mine. "And how do you feel about playing host to such a pivotal event in the festival? There's a lot riding on tonight, not least of which is Books and Brew's reputation as a cultural hub. I also heard there are some financial implications for your little store."

My *little* store? It took every fiber in my being to stay controlled by Sophie's casual putdown. I took a deep breath, confused about how she knew anything about my monetary struggles. After my grandma passed away and deeded me the store, I discovered it was deep in the red. Desperate to save it, I pooled funds with an old flame to remortgage, but he left me high and dry making things even worse. "Books and Brew has always been more than just a bookstore or café. It's a place where people can come together to share, learn, and grow. We are thrilled to host the kickoff lecture this evening."

Sophie nodded, her pen pausing for a moment. "It's certainly a night to remember. Thanks, I'll make sure this story gets the spotlight it deserves."

As she melted back into the crowd, I returned to Zoe and Lottie, a sense of accomplishment mingling with the nerves. "That's going to be one interesting article," I said, allowing myself a moment to bask in the excitement.

Lottie chuckled, patting me on the back. "You handled that like a pro. Now, let's make sure the rest of the night goes off without a hitch."

Just then, a hush fell over the crowd as Professor Emerson made his way to the front, his presence commanding attention even before he'd spoken a word. "Looks like it's showtime," I murmured, sharing a look with Zoe and Lottie.

As the Professor cleared his throat, preparing to begin, the room's anticipation reached its zenith, everyone clinging to the promise of secrets about to be unearthed, all within the walls of Books and Brew.

Professor Emerson, standing confidently before the captivated audience, wove a narrative that hinted at the depth of his discoveries. "In my recent research," he started, his voice measured to draw in the crowd. "I've encountered evidence that challenges some of our long-held beliefs about Maplebrook's early days. Specifically, the roles played by certain influential figures in shaping our town's destiny." He paused, letting the implication of his words hang in the air.

Whispers spread through the room like ripples in a pond as the audience processed his hint of controversy.

"While the full scope of my findings will be detailed in my forthcoming paper," he continued. "I can share with you tonight that our town's history might not be as straightforward as we've been led to believe. For instance, consider the widely-celebrated story of Maplebrook's founding. Our narrative has always glorified the unity and shared vision of our forebears. However, hidden within the pages of long-forgotten diaries and correspondence, I've uncovered hints of deep-seated rivalries, secret agreements, and even betrayal."

The room was electric with curiosity, attendees leaning forward, hungry for more.

"Take, for example, the supposed harmony between the town's founding families. This, too, might be more myth than reality. What if I told you that beneath the facade of collaboration lay a web of deceit spun from greed and a ruthless pursuit of power?"

Murmurs filled the room, a mixture of intrigue and disbelief.

"Of course," Professor Emerson quickly added. "These findings are preliminary. They raise as many questions as they answer. In the days ahead, I hope to verify these suspicions and bring the full truth to light. For now, let us consider tonight's discussion a...prelude to a larger conversation about our town's history, one that I look forward to continuing with all of you."

"Let us all be mindful of the stories we inherit and the histories we construct," Professor Emerson intoned, a mischievous glint in his eye. "Sometimes, the truth isn't buried in the ground but hidden within the pages, waiting for someone daring enough to read between the lines. Beware, my friends. The seemingly innocuous tales of our past might just hold the explosive tales of our future. And trust me. The real mysteries lie not in what is said, but in what is purposely left out."

As the applause softened and the room filled with the hum of excited conversations, I leaned closer to Zoe, ensuring our whispered exchange remained just between us amid the post-lecture buzz. "Betrayal and secret agreements, huh?" I murmured, my voice laced with intrigue. "Emerson's on to something big, isn't he?"

As the last of the guests filtered out of Books and Brew, their conversations still buzzing with theories and speculation, I began tidying up. Jazz prowled between chairs and tables, inspecting each corner as if to ensure no crumb or secret had been left behind.

"Quite the night, huh, Jazzalicious?" I said, stacking chairs and wiping down tables. "Maplebrook will talk about this one for a while."

Jazz meowed softly in response, his green eyes tracking my every move as if to offer his support—or perhaps just waiting for the chance to curl up in my lap once the work was done.

As I made my way towards the back of the store to retrieve a broom, my thoughts wandered, replaying snippets of Professor Emerson's talk. The potential implications of his findings on Maplebrook's history were both thrilling and daunting. Lost in thought, I almost didn't notice the anomaly in the shadows near the back where the soft evening light failed to reach.

That's when I saw it. Or rather, him.

There, slumped over a table at the back of the shop, was Professor Emerson, motionless, his face eerily still in the dim light. His lecture notes were scattered around him, a testament to the evening's excitement now turned somber, and his tea had spilled, the dark stain seeping into the fabric of the tablecloth.

Professor Emerson was dead.

Chapter Three

♥

The morning sun streamed through the windows of Books and Brew, casting a warm glow over the crime scene tape now marring the cozy ambiance of my bookstore. Jazz sat perched atop a nearby shelf, his eyes tracking every newcomer with feline skepticism.

The buzz of speculation and concern from the crowd outside had yet to penetrate the quiet stillness of the shop's interior, making Detective Luke Harper's entrance more pronounced. From what I understood, he was new to Maplebrook, a transfer to our small town after some recent retirements and promotions. To be honest, I didn't follow our local law enforcement too closely. We didn't have much crime in our little town, but if the head detective looked like this guy, I might take more of an interest.

Detective Harper was tall and fit, with wavy, black hair and piercing blue eyes which seemed to miss nothing. Dressed in well-fitting jeans and a dark shirt, he seemed to balance professional and approachable. My heart did a little pitter-pat.

"Piper Page?" he asked, extending his hand, though the solemnity of the situation kept our handshake brief and formal.

"That's me," I replied, attempting to mask the turmoil of emotions with a semblance of composure. "You must be Detective Harper."

"We're pretty informal around here. You can call me Luke." He pulled a small notebook from his pocket. "I understand you found the body?"

"Yes, I did," I replied, my voice steady, despite the tumultuous fear swirling within me. "Just after the lecture. Everyone had left, and I was cleaning up. That's when I—" My explanation was cut short by Zoe's dramatic entrance, who burst through the door like a whirlwind of panic and disarray.

"Pipes!" she exclaimed, wide-eyed and breathless. "You won't believe what I just heard-"

Luke and I exchanged a glance, the seriousness of our conversation momentarily derailed.

"Zoe, this is Detective Harper. Luke. He's here about Professor Emerson," I said, introducing them, but quickly trying to steer the conversation back to the matter at hand.

" Detective, hi!" Zoe managed, her expression shifting from shock to embarrassment in a heartbeat. "I didn't mean to barge in. I just heard about the Professor and came rushing over. Piper, are you okay?"

I couldn't help but smile sadly at Zoe's concern, her frenzied energy momentarily lifting the gravity of the situation. "I'm okay. Thanks for checking in. The detective was just asking about last night."

"It's alright, Zoe," Luke chimed in. He'd been observing the exchange with an amused yet patient look. "If you were here last night as well, I'd like to hear anything you might have to say, too. Every detail helps."

Zoe nodded, seemingly grounding herself at the mention of contributing to the investigation. "Of course, anything to help. But, Piper here, she's the one with the eagle eye. She remembers everything, like where every single guest was sitting and what they were drinking!"

Luke shifted his gaze back to me. "Is that so? Quite impressive. Your recollection could be invaluable to the case."

I felt a blush creep up my cheeks, not used to being on the receiving end of such praise, especially under such frightening circumstances. "I guess I just pay attention to the details," I said modestly, hoping my memory could indeed help bring some clarity to the tragic events of the night.

Luke leaned in, his interest clearly piqued by the potential insights my observations could provide. "Piper, could you go over any specifics from last night that caught your attention?"

I did a double-take. "Wait a minute. Are you suggesting that the Professor's death wasn't by natural causes?" I'd assumed when I found him slumped over, he'd had a heart attack or stroke or something. But if Luke was here, asking about specifics, then that meant –

"I can't share the details of an ongoing investigation, but the coroner hasn't ruled out foul play," Luke confirmed.

Murder? At Books and Brew?

This was very, very bad.

"Piper?" Luke touched my arm, bringing me out of my own thoughts. "Is there anything about last night that you can remember? Anything you think might be helpful?"

Helpful to a murder investigation? I was a bookstore owner, not a detective. I took a deep breath, trying to think of something useful. "There was one thing...when I was closing up, I did feel a chill in the air...like the back door had been opened. But we don't use that door, especially when we have events. I don't see any reason for it to have been used at all during the lecture." I paused for a moment, remembering. "That's where I found the Professor...at a table near the back door."

It was at this moment, Zoe burst back into the conversation, her usual energy bringing a spark even to the serious discussion. "Oh! That reminds me. I thought I saw a shadow moving at the back during the discussion. I figured it was just someone stepping out quietly, but now, thinking about it, it seems odd."

Before we could delve deeper into Zoe's observation, Lottie breezed in, the chime of the door heralding her arrival. She paused, taking in our huddled group. "If it isn't Maplebrook's finest. You should see the crowd outside, buzzing like bees around your crime scene tape. It's like we're hosting the town's most morbid book club." Her attempt to lighten the mood with her signature blend of humor and observation was appreciated, even if it couldn't entirely dispel the tension in the air.

After a brief update, she mused on our observations. "Strange about the back door. I did hear something like a door gently closing. Thought it was just the wind or my imagination."

Luke's attention shifted between us, his detective's mind piecing together the fragments of our shared experiences. "It sounds like we have a potential unaccounted visitor during the lecture. These details about the back door could be crucial."

Zoe leaned against the counter, her brow furrowed. "Do you think someone was there, listening in? Someone who didn't want to be seen?"

"It's a possibility we can't ignore," Luke admitted, his tone serious.

"Piper, tell him about the note," Zoe nudged.

Luke's gaze shifted towards me at Zoe's suggestion, a mixture of professional curiosity and personal concern evident in his expression. "Note?" he inquired.

Taking a deep breath, I reached into my pocket, pulling out the crumpled piece of paper which had started it all. Handing it over to

Luke, I watched his eyes scan the hastily-written message, his brow furrowing as he absorbed its contents.

"It was left for me," I explained, my voice tinged with unease. "I found it the morning of the lecture. It didn't make much sense then, but now..."

Luke's expression darkened, the note in his hand suddenly seeming to carry more weight. "This changes things," he said slowly. "It suggests that Professor Emerson's lecture—and possibly Emerson himself—was targeted. And if someone's going to the lengths of leaving anonymous warnings, it's serious."

Zoe looked from Luke to me, her concern deepening. " Piper really could be in danger? What should we do?"

Luke met my gaze, his eyes conveying a determination that was somehow reassuring. "We'll increase patrols around Books and Brew, for starters. Piper, I want you to be extra-vigilant and report any-thing—no matter how insignificant — that feels out of the ordinary."

"On the bright side, it seems Books and Brew is the place to be for all the action," Lottie chimed in with her characteristic blend of humor and practicality after quietly absorbing the conversation. "Though I'd prefer a book club meeting to a murder investigation as our next big event."

Despite the gravity of the situation, her comment elicited a brief, collective chuckle, breaking the tension for a moment. "Thank you, Lottie," Luke said with a small smile, appreciating the light moment before turning back to me. "Piper, I'm going to need to keep the note. It could be a key piece of evidence. But don't worry; we're going to get to the bottom of all of this."

"Of course," I replied, passing it over with a sense of relinquishing not just the paper, but a piece of the puzzle that had turned Books and Brew—and my life—upside down. Luke's reassurance, coupled with his reassuring expression, offered a glimmer of hope in the shadow of the mystery.

Just then, Jazz, who had been silently observing the exchange from his perch on a nearby shelf, gave a soft purr, as if casting his vote of confidence in Luke's ability to unravel the tangled web of secrets and lies. Zoe, catching Jazz's quiet endorsement, couldn't help smile. "If Jazz approves, I suppose we're in good hands." She showed a twinkle of amusement in her eyes.

I chuckled, grateful for the moment of levity. "Between Luke's detective skills and Jazz's seal of approval, how can we go wrong?" I said, smiling at Luke. "We're all looking forward to putting this behind us."

Luke cleared his throat. "Your store is going to have to stay closed for the next 24 hours while CSI finishes their investigation. They need time to gather fingerprints, hair, fur, and other DNA samples."

My heart sank. Another day closed meant more financial strain. "Of course. Whatever you need to do."

Inside, my mind race. How was I going to manage this. The bills were piling up, and every day closed was a day closer to sinking deep into the red. But I couldn't let Lottie see my worry. I had to stay strong, for the store and for my grandmother's legacy.

After the detective left, I turned to Zoe. "Alright, don't you have a gallery to enchant with your presence today?" I nudged her gently as we straightened the chairs and laid out fresh pastries. Zoe flashed me a grin, her hands momentarily pausing in their work.

"What, and miss the opportunity to play detective with you here? The gallery can wait. Besides, you need someone to keep your sleuthing instincts in check. And," she added with a grin. "Maybe talk about that cute detective?"

"So you're my voice of reason now? That's rich," I said, unable to suppress a smile, despite the situation. "This coming from the woman who once chased down a so-called 'haunted' ice cream truck because it played a different tune. Your free spirit knows no bounds, Zoe." I shook my head. "I'm not interested in Luke or any other guy right now. I'm only focused on the store."

The next morning, the usual rush of customers was conspicuously absent, and my worry about the murder's impact on the store gnawed at me. Among the few who ventured in was Dean Foster, curator of the Maplebrook Historical Museum. He was a regular, known for his dual passion for our coffee and the pulse of local gossip. Seeing him stride in with his familiar inquisitive glint gave me a small sense of normalcy.

"Dean," I greeted him, bringing over a cup of his favorite espresso. "I was shocked we didn't see you at the lecture the other night. It was right up your alley—full of historical twists and turns."

Dean's face was a mix of casual dismissal and genuine regret. " I heard it was quite the event. Unfortunately, museum duties called—had an unexpected situation to handle." He paused to brush some dust off his jacket sleeve, which struck me as odd since Dean was usually so meticulous about his appearance. "Just terrible news about the Professor. What's the inside scoop?"

My spidey senses tingled as I took in Dean's reaction. He was unusually nonchalant, considering how close he was to the Professor. Why would he miss a lecture from his favorite speaker? And why was he so curious now?

I felt prickle of unease as I glanced around the nearly empty shop. "It's been a whirlwind. I'm just hoping people aren't too spooked to come back."

Dean nodded sympathetically, but I noticed a flicker of something else in his eyes. "These things have a way of blowing over, but I'm here for my daily dose of espresso and gossip."

Lottie, ever the diplomat, offered him a smile. "No scoop from us lowly bookshop keepers, Dean. Just the usual intrigue. You know, mystery, suspense, the occasional deadly plot twist."

Dean took a sip of his coffee and then raised his cup. "Keep me in the loop. A good thriller's always worth sticking around for."

As he settled into his favorite spot, I caught Zoe's eye, sharing a silent agreement that, despite the levity, the day ahead promised its own share of mysteries. My gaze fell upon the guest sign-in book from the lecture, left open on the counter. My heart skipped a beat as I noticed something amiss—a page torn out. "Zoe, look," I murmured, drawing her attention to the book.

Her playful demeanor faded, replaced by a spark of curiosity. "A missing page? That's...oddly convenient, don't you think?"

I nodded, a sense of unease settling over me. Had the murderer really been in my shop? Maybe standing right next to me? The thought of it made me frightened. "Too convenient. Looks like our little detective game just got its first real clue."

Zoe's eyes sparkled with excitement. "Oh, we're like amateur sleuths now, aren't we? Next, you'll be telling me you've got a deerstalker hat stashed away for just such an occasion."

Before I could retort, Jazz, our unofficial third detective, sauntered over, a streak of dirt adorning his otherwise-pristine white and black fur. "And what mysteries have you been uncovering, hmm?" I asked him, bending down to inspect his nose. Jazz simply purred, oblivious to the significance of his appearance. Zoe leaned in, her gaze following mine. "Since when does Jazz play in the dirt? He's the most indoorsy cat I know."

"Exactly," I said, straightening up to scan the room.

Jazz seemed perfectly content with the dirt smudging his white and black fur. "Jazz, show me where you got your nose dirty," I said, half-joking, yet curious if the adventurous cat might unknowingly lead us to another clue.

Zoe watched as Jazz simply purred in response, clearly uninterested in leading any sort of investigation. "Wouldn't it be something if Jazz turned out to be our secret detective?" she mused.

Jazz, perhaps sensing our focus on him or simply deciding it was time for his own exploration, began to saunter towards the back of the store. We exchanged a glance, curiosity rising by the cat's sudden interest in the rear of the shop, a place he usually frequented less.

"Looks like he's taking up the detective mantle after all," I joked, following Jazz's lead with Zoe close behind. As Jazz made his way to the back door, he paused, sitting with a peculiar attentiveness only cats seem to master.

It was there, right where Jazz had stopped and seemed to be scrutinizing the floor. A faint but undeniable footprint near the door, partially obscured by the usual backroom clutter which had been hastily rearranged in the aftermath of the previous day's events. "I can't believe this," Zoe whispered, crouching down for a closer look. "Jazz actually found something." I knelt beside her, examining the print. It was too distinct to be anything but recent, and its location suggested someone might have indeed used the back door, either during or after the lecture—a detail that had gone unnoticed until now.

"Detective Jazz, on the case," I said, a smile touching my lips despite the gravity of our discovery. "But really, this could be a crucial piece of evidence. The back door...I didn't even consider it before."

Zoe looked up from the footprint, her eyes meeting mine. "We need to tell Luke about this. Whoever left this print might know more about what happened to Professor Emerson." Jazz, pleased with his contribution, simply sat and watched us, his tail flicking lightly. Zoe's suggestion hung in the air, a silent acknowledgment of the gravity of our discovery. "You're right," I conceded, feeling the weight of responsibility settle over us. "This could be the breakthrough Luke needs. We can't keep this to ourselves."

Chapter Four

♥

"Lottie, would you mind covering Books and Brew for a bit? I need to head to the police station," I said, trying to mask the urgency in my voice with a casualness I didn't feel.

Lottie looked up from her task of rearranging the mystery section, a place which now felt all too relevant. "Off to see our detective friend?" she teased, her tone light. "Don't do anything I wouldn't do."

I managed a half-smile. "Just need to share some findings. That footprint and the missing page from the sign-in book might be more important than we thought."

Her nod was all the encouragement I needed. With Lottie's assurance Books and Brew was in capable hands, I stepped out for a short walk to the local police department. Stepping into the quiet, almost serene atmosphere of the small-town police station, the contrast to the bustling city precincts I'd seen on TV was stark. The place was laid-back, with just a few officers going about their tasks unhurriedly. There, behind the reception desk, was Ruby Harrison, my mother's best friend and the station's dispatcher. Known for her warmth and ready smile, Ruby had a knack for making everyone feel at ease, a touch of homeliness in the formal setting.

"Ruby!" I called out, making my way over to her desk, cluttered with files but also adorned with personal touches, making it unmistakably hers. I hated to admit it, but I was hoping I could use our personal relationship to get some inside information. Turns out I didn't have to try too hard.

"Piper, darling!" Ruby waved and greeted me with a warmth which could melt the coldest of cases.

Before I could dive into the reason for my visit, Ruby leaned in, her voice dropping to a conspiratorial whisper. "Listen, you didn't hear it from me, but there's been a development in the Professor's case. They found out he was poisoned."

The news hit me like a ton of bricks. *Poisoned*? The revelation the poisoning might have happened at my store sent a shiver of worry through me.

"Poisoned?" I repeated, trying to keep my reaction measured, though my mind raced with the implications. While I felt terrible for the Professor, I also had to worry about how this news was going to affect the festival and my business financially. "That's-- that's huge. Do they have any leads on how or why?"

Ruby glanced around before leaning in closer, the buzz of the station around us fading into the background as her words took center stage. "Nothing concrete yet, but you know how it is—rumors are flying. Luke's been on edge, more so than usual. They're keeping it under wraps until they know more."

I nodded, processing the information. Ruby, as always, was a wellspring of insights, her position within the station giving her access to tidbits of information which were gold for someone like me.

"Thanks, Ruby," I said, my mind already turning over the new information. "I wanted to see Luke about something I found at Books and Brew. Is he available?"

Ruby, eager to assist, reached for her phone and buzzed his office. Moments later, he emerged, his expression one of heated irritation.

"Detective Harper, uh, Luke," I began, forcing my voice to remain steady despite the flutter of nerves in my stomach. "I found something at my store you need to see. I think it could be important."

"Ah, Piper. Just the person I wanted to see," Luke said, his demeanor serious. "We've just received the toxicology report on the Professor's tea. It confirms he was poisoned."

My heart skipped a beat. "Poisoned? But how—" I stopped myself, not wanting to clue Luke in on how Ruby had already whispered the toxicology results to me in confidence.

Luke's gaze sharpened. "Piper, did you serve him the drink?"

I felt a cold wave of shock wash over me. "What? No! I mean, yes, I served him, but I would never—"

His eyes were unwavering, making my pulse race. "You have to understand how this looks. You had access to the drinks. It's your store."

Offended, scared, and with a hint of desperation, I protested, "I would never harm anyone, let alone the Professor. Books and Brew is my life. I need to know who did this as much as you do. Please, you have to believe me."

He studied me for a long moment, his expression softening slightly. "Honestly, I'd be surprised if you did it. But I have to follow every lead. Show me what you found at the store. Maybe it can help clear your name."

I nodded, swallowing hard. "Thank you. I just want to help find the real culprit and clear this cloud hanging over Books and Brew."

As we stepped back into Books and Brew, I led Luke to the secluded part of the bookstore where I'd discovered the footprint. I couldn't wait to tell him he missed the torn-out page in my guest book. "Here,"

I said, pointing to the floor. The footprint was still there, faint but unmistakable against the dark wood. "I found it after everyone had left. Actually, Jazz found it. And like I said, that area had been cleaned before the lecture. No one had any reason to be back here."

Luke knelt down for a closer look, his expression shifting from skepticism to contemplation. "You're right," he admitted after a moment. "This couldn't have been from earlier in the day. And it's too far from the main area to be accidental."

I thought about saying "I told you so," but decided not to push my luck. Instead, I watched him, a small sense of vindication growing inside me. "Does this mean you're starting to believe that I might actually be helpful in the investigation?"

He stood up, dusting off his hands. He met my gaze with a look somewhere between annoyance and acknowledgment, but I didn't care, as long as he was listening to what I had to say. "Don't push your luck, Piper. But yes, this is...useful. And I suppose I have you to thank for not letting it go unnoticed."

"See? Bookstore owner by day, amateur detective by... also day," I said, unable to resist the opportunity for a little more banter.

Luke shook his head, a half-smile betraying his attempt to remain all business. "Just don't quit your day job, okay? We'll need to get this processed. If we can get a match for the print, it could be a significant lead."

As he pulled out his phone to call it in, I allowed myself an infinitesimal moment of satisfaction. Luke was seeing my familiarity with Books and Brew and its customers could offer insights beyond the reach of standard police procedure. It was a small step toward building trust, but still progress. And in a case as tangled as this, any advancement counted.

"Alright, Luke," I said, after he ended his call. "Let's see where this clue leads us. Just remember, I'm full of surprises."

He laughed. "I'm not sure how many surprises I can take."

With a mock salute and a playful glint in my eye, I turned back to the task at hand. But before diving back into the world of missing pages and mysterious footprints, I scooped up Jazz, who had been an attentive audience to our entire exchange. Holding him close, I whispered, "Looks like we're both on detective duty now, buddy."

The literary festival was in full swing the next day. I made my way to Palette Whispers, Zoe's eclectic art shop as it stood vibrant and inviting against the morning light. The Art and Literature Exhibition was one of the main events of the festival, and Zoe's contributions were always a highlight.

"Zoe!" I greeted as I stepped into the kaleidoscope of colors which was her shop. "I'm here for the art pieces for the exhibition at Books and Brew. Ready to dazzle us with your latest masterpieces?"

Zoe emerged from behind a canvas, her hands stained wet with splashes of red and purple paint, a wide grin on her face. "You came just in time! I've got a few pieces that'll knock your literary socks off. Inspired by our favorite books, of course."

She led me through the shop, pointing out each piece with the enthusiasm of a genuine artist. "This one," she gestured to a vibrant painting which somehow perfectly captured the essence of "The Great Gatsby". "It is all about the decadence and disillusionment of the Jazz Age. And this,--" she moved to a hauntingly beautiful portrayal of the moors from "Wuthering Heights". "--Captures Cathy's wild spirit and the desolate beauty of the landscape."

I was genuinely impressed. "These are incredible. The way you've brought the stories to life - I can just see the characters leap off the page and onto the canvas."

She beamed, clearly proud of her work. "That's the idea! I want people to really *feel* the stories, to see them in a new light. Art and literature, they're two sides of the same coin, really."

We chatted a bit more about the pieces, Zoe explaining her process and inspiration with a passion which was infectious. If I had an artistic bone in my body, I'd be jealous of her talent. But ultimately, I was really so proud to call her my best friend. "These are going to be a hit at the exhibition. You've really outdone yourself this year."

Zoe shrugged modestly, a playful spark in her eyes. "You know me. It's not a festival without a little flair, right?"

As I made my move to leave Palette Whispers, Zoe's voice halted me in my tracks. "Before you go, did you catch Sophie's latest editorial masterpiece? She's casting some serious shade on Emerson's so-called, earth-shattering revelations."

I spun around, eyes wide. "What? I haven't seen the paper yet this morning. Let me guess, she thinks Emerson's big reveal was about discovering some long-lost treasure hidden beneath Maplebrook?"

Zoe snorted, holding up the paper with a flourish. "Close, but no cigar. She's insinuating that Emerson's 'pending revelations' might have been more about stirring the pot than unearthing any real dirt. Basically, she was questioning if our beloved professor was the literary world's equivalent of a conspiracy theorist."

I grabbed the paper, scanning the article with a frown. "Wow, Sophie's really going for the Pulitzer with this one. Next, she'll be saying Emerson was about to disclose that Maplebrook is built on an ancient alien landing site."

"Or that he found proof the town library is secretly a gateway to Narnia." Zoe leaned closer, rolling her eyes. "Honestly, Piper, how did we miss these signs?"

With a dramatic sigh, I folded the paper and tucked it under my arm with the artwork. "Clearly, we've been slacking on our duties as Maplebrook's premier cultural detectives. We should be on the lookout for mysterious wardrobes and unexplained crop circles."

Zoe's laughter followed me to the door. "Just be sure to keep an eye out for any secret meetings of the Illuminati in the Self Help section."

"Will do," I giggled, giving her a wave as I left.

As I made my way back to Books and Brew, navigating through the bustling streets filled with festival-goers and the vibrant energy of Maplebrook in full literary bloom, I nearly bumped into Ethan Hargrove. Ethan, known in town for his philanthropy as much as his keen interest in the arts, was this year's sponsor for a significant portion of the festival. "I didn't expect to see you here," I said, a bit startled by the sudden encounter.

Ethan offered a charming smile. "Good to see you. I wouldn't miss the festival for the world, especially not when I have the honor of sponsoring it. How are things at Books and Brew? I heard about the unfortunate incident with Professor Emerson."

The mention of Professor Emerson brought a sobering note to our light-hearted festival atmosphere. "It's been a challenging time," I admitted. "But we're trying to keep the festival moving forward, in honor of the Professor and his love for history and literature."

"That's the spirit," Ethan replied, admiration clear in his bright eyes as he gently took my hand. "Maplebrook needs more people like you, Piper. Your dedication to blending literature and community is exactly why I support the festival. It's more than just an event; it's a celebration of what makes our town unique."

I felt a flush of pride and appreciation at his words. "Thanks, Ethan. That really means a lot."

Ethan nodded, a thoughtful look crossing his features. "If there's anything I can do to help, ask. But if you'll excuse me, I have a few more people to greet before the day gets away from me."

Energized by Ethan's offer of support and the lively spirit of the festival thrumming through the streets of Maplebrook, I made my way back to Books and Brew, arms heavy with Zoe's vibrant artwork. The morning's events had left me with a mixed bag of emotions, but the task at hand offered a welcome distraction.

"Ah, the prodigal art curator returns," Lottie joked, wiping her hands on her apron as she came over to help me. "These look amazing. Zoe's outdone herself this year."

"I know, right?" I replied, weaving through the few customers scattered around the store to place the pieces carefully on a nearby table. "We were saying how art and literature are just two sides of the same coin. It's going to be a grand exhibition."

As we set up Zoe's paintings around Books and Brew, arranging pieces next to their literary inspirations, our conversation flowed easily from the festival's events to the more pressing matter which lingered at the back of our minds—the mystery surrounding Professor Emerson's death.

"You know," Lottie said, studying a painting inspired by <u>Jane Eyre</u>. "With all this talk about art imitating life, it's hard not to think about the story unfolding right here. It's like we're living in our own mystery novel."

I chuckled, though the comparison felt all too apt. "Let's just hope for a happier ending than some of the books on our shelves. And speaking of stories, Ethan Hargrove stopped me on my way back here. You know he's one of the festival sponsors? Anyway, he said if we needed anything to let him know."

Lottie raised her eyebrows, impressed. "Ethan's backing? That could come in handy, for sure. That guy has more money and influence than about anyone else in town."

"Yeah," I mused, straightening a framed illustration of *The Secret Garden*. "Could come in handy if our sales start to tank after...well, you know. Either people are going to avoid the scene of a murder investigation like the plague, or they'll flock to us."

With the artwork in place, Books and Brew transformed into a visual homage to the written word. Lottie and I took a step back to admire our handiwork.

"Alright, Detective Page," Lottie teased, pulling me from my thoughts. "Fingers crossed. Let's get this place ready for the crowd."

Chapter Five

♥

The Lazy Llama, nestled in the heart of Maplebrook, was a cozy Mexican restaurant famed for its vibrant decor, featuring walls adorned with colorful llama paintings and warm, inviting lighting. It was intimate yet lively, a go-to for locals craving delicious cuisine. The aroma of spices and the sound of laughter filled the air, creating a comforting backdrop for its customers.

As Zoe and I savored our lunch, the hum of conversations and clinking of dishes gradually faded into the background. Just then, Margie, my loud, over-the-top, and well-meaning mother, entered with a group of friends in tow. When she spotted us, she bee-lined to our table, her entourage forming a lively backdrop. "Piper, darling!" she exclaimed, her eyes alight with excitement and the latest gossip she couldn't wait to share. "Ruby just told me you're getting involved with the case. And with that cute new detective, no less."

Before I could muster a response, she leaned in. "You know, I heard he's single, and so are you," she said, her voice dropping to a conspiratorial whisper.

I couldn't help but roll my eyes, a response honed from years of similar nudges and winks about my personal life. "Mom," I sighed, a blend of affection and mild frustration coloring my voice. "Can we not do this here?"

Unfazed by my plea, my mother gently patted my hand and winked. "Just saying, Dear. You never know where or when you'll find love. Or how!" She returned to her friends, her departure marked by a trail of chuckles and amused glances from nearby diners.

Zoe, having quietly enjoyed the exchange, chimed in with a wide grin. "Your mom never misses a beat, does she?"

Shaking my head, I allowed a smile to break through. "Never," I conceded, appreciating the mix of meddling and care characterizing my mother's approach to life. "But maybe, just maybe, she could take a tiny step back from playing matchmaker. Luke isn't my type, anyway," I mused, hoping to steer the conversation away from the choppy waters of my non-existent love life.

Zoe pondered for a moment, a playful challenge lighting up her eyes. "Tall, dark, and handsome isn't your type?" She was obviously enjoying the moment.

"He's dismissive and rude," I countered, emphasizing my point with a bite of my taco. "Besides, a relationship is the last thing I want right now. I've got enough on my plate. I'd rather focus on chips and salsa."

Just as we were settling back into our lunch, the door to The Lazy Llama swung open, admitting another well-known figure into the mix. Sophie, with her knack for turning every tidbit of Maplebrook news into front-page material, strolled in, her eyes scanning the room until they landed on us.

"Great," I muttered under my breath, catching my friend's eye. "Can't we just eat our meal in peace?"

But peace, it seemed, was too much to ask for in a town like Maplebrook where every meal could easily turn into an impromptu meeting or the spark of a new lead. Sophie's determined approach signaled the end of our brief respite and the beginning of yet another conversation I had hoped to avoid—at least until after lunch.

"Sophie," I greeted with a casual nod as she approached our table, her latest journalistic adventure folded under her arm. "I read your article on Professor Emerson. I thought I was reading a script for a soap opera. Any plans to pivot to daytime TV?"

Sophie slid into the seat across from us, the ghost of a smirk playing on her lips. "Come on now, Piper. Emerson's research was too juicy not to dive into."

Zoe barely suppressed a chuckle.

"It was certainly...intriguing," I conceded. "Though I half-expected to find out he was secretly Batman by the end."

Zoe, seizing the baton of our impromptu comedy duo, nudged Sophie. "Or maybe that he'd cracked the code to eternal youth. We could all use a bit of that, couldn't we?"

Sophie leaned back, amusement flickering in her eyes as she considered our banter. "You two should take your act on the road. But seriously, with everything going on, a little speculation keeps things interesting."

I took a thoughtful bite of my taco, musing over her words. "Speculation keeps the wheels turning, but so does digging deeper. Maybe next time, a follow-up piece? The truth is often stranger than fiction, after all."

Sophie tossed a newspaper onto the table and tapped a perfectly-manicured nail on the headline. "Speaking of follow-up pieces, maybe you've seen my article on Charlie Alderton today?"

Sophie's sudden shift caught me mid-chew, a tactic I recognized and respected in equal measure. Her mention of Charlie Alderton, a name which buzzed with its own set of rumors and whispers around Maplebrook, piqued my interest instantly. I set my taco down, my appetite momentarily forgotten, and picked up the newspaper she had casually tossed our way. The headline was bold, designed to catch the eye and hold it captive: *Charlie Alderton: Maplebrook's Hidden Gem or Forgotten Folly?*

"Moving from academia to local legends, are we?" I mused, glancing up at Sophie.

Sophie's smile was enigmatic, a clear sign she believed she was onto something. "Everyone loves a good mystery. And Charlie's story? It's ripe for the picking. There's more to him than most people remember."

Zoe leaned over to get a better look at the article, her curiosity visibly piqued. "I've heard bits and pieces, but nothing concrete. What's the angle, Sophie?"

Sophie, with a sparkle in her eye that could rival the most seasoned storytellers, leaned closer, lowering her voice as though she were about to share the secret to an ancient mystery. "He isn't just another character in Maplebrook's ongoing saga. He's a direct link to the founding families, practically royalty here. And his showdown with Emerson? Picture it—a clash not just of opinions, but of eras." Her enthusiasm was palpable, her storytelling engaging, drawing us into the heart of the drama with the finesse of a practiced journalist. "Their public disputes were legendary."

Sophie allowed the weight of her words to sink in, her demeanor reflective of someone who relished the unfolding of a good plot. "What do you think? Emerson's research threatened to upend the Alderton family name. It's not just a story—it's a powder keg waiting for a spark."

With a final, dramatic flourish, she stood up, leaving Zoe and me to contemplate the intricate web of history and mystery she had spun.

"Keep your eyes open," she advised with a wink. "In Maplebrook, the past isn't just history; it's the key to the present."

After a busy afternoon, the day had drawn to a close, and I was grateful. During the last few hours, all I could really think about was turning on some good music and slipping into a bubble bath. Maybe pouring a glass of wine and having the last slice of Evie's banana bread that was still lingering in the front bakery case. I told myself it would probably be too dry to sell by tomorrow, so I should spare serving subpar goodies to my customers. I'd take one for the team.

This place was more than a bookstore to me; it was my sanctuary. At Books and Brew, stories lived and breathed, and one could shelve the weight of the world, if only for a while. I wanted the same feeling for my customers, for people who picked up a book and got lost in their own world of stories and make-believe. My place of solitude and comfort had been the scene of a murder less than twenty-four hours didn't make me frightened. It made me angry.

I wasn't easily scared, and I had my grandma to thank for that. In her youth, she was the adventurous one, always off on some wild escapade—traveling to exotic places or sailing the open seas before she settled down and opened Books and Brew with my grandfather. He was the solid rock to her whirlwind, always supporting her fearless spirit. She passed that same spirit on to me. Back in school, I once stood up to a bully twice my size who was picking on a friend. Fear wasn't something I entertained; it was something I confronted. And now, with my bookstore at the center of a murder investigation, I felt that same defiant courage rising within me. I was determined to uncover the truth and protect the sanctuary that my grandma had entrusted to me.

I lingered after locking the door, savoring the solitude, the way the dimmed lights cast shadows between the aisles, each book a silent sentinel in the gathering dusk.

"One more day conquered, Jazz," I murmured, glancing at the tuxedo cat sprawled across the counter, his green eyes reflecting the muted light like twin emeralds.

Jazz merely blinked, his tail flicking in what I imagined was agreement. If only I felt as relaxed as he did.

While I was cleaning up, I couldn't help but think about the mystery surrounding Maplebook after Professor Emerson's death. It felt personal, a story unfolding too close to home, with unwritten chapters which felt threatening.

That's when I saw it.

Lying just outside the front door, as though it had been waiting for me, was a book. Not just any book, but a first edition of <u>The Secret History</u>, its cover bathed in the soft glow of the streetlight seeping through the glass. My breath caught, heart pounding against my ribs like a caged bird. This wasn't just a misplaced volume; it was a message.

I picked up the book, my fingers tracing the familiar spine. I turned to Jazz, who had roused himself from his repose, watching me with an intensity which belied his usual indifference. "Looks like our quiet evening just got a lot more interesting," I said, trying to infuse my voice with a bravado I didn't really feel.

Opening the book, the mark on the title page sent a chill down my spine—a circle with a line through it, an eye crossed out. It was a symbol I didn't recognize, but its intention was clear. A warning. A threat, tied to the very core of what made Books and Brew—and me—what we were. Literature, history, and the pursuit of truth.

"Why would someone do this, Jazz?" I whispered, half-expecting the cat to offer some nugget of wisdom, to unravel the mystery with a flick of his tail. Instead, he simply jumped down from the counter, padding over to nuzzle against my leg, a silent show of solidarity.

I knelt beside him; the book clutched in my hand, and allowed myself a moment of vulnerability. "They're trying to scare us, Jazz. To keep us from finding out the truth about Professor Emerson. But this--" I gestured to the book, to the mark which had turned a treasure into a taunt. "--this only makes me want to dig deeper."

The cat, in a way only cats seemed capable of, demonstrated his understanding by purring gently, offering comfort. It was a reminder that even in the face of unseen threats, I wasn't alone. I had Jazz; I had Zoe and Lottie, and I had Books and Brew.

With a renewed sense of determination, I stood, placing *The Secret History* back on its shelf. "We won't be intimidated," I declared to the empty room, to Jazz, to the night itself. I grabbed that chocolate cake and headed up the stairs, Jazz hot at my heels. "We'll find the answers, Professor. I promise."

Chapter Six

♥

The morning sun snuck in, gently nudging me awake with a reminder that, yes, the world kept spinning even after I discovered creepy symbols in my favorite books. My loft, perched above Books and Brew, was cluttered with artifacts of my many interests—each book, each oddity, serving as a testament to a life lived with curiosity. Jazz, my partner in crime-solving (or at least in living), watched with his usual feline amusement as I shuffled about, half-awake, feeding him his gourmet breakfast. It was no exaggeration the cat ate better than I did.

I scratched behind his ears. "Top of the morning to you. Ready to tackle the mysteries of the universe? Or just the litter box?" I said, trying not to let the weight of last night's discoveries dampen the start of a new day.

Armed with a mug of strong coffee and wearing my favorite graphic tee with a quirky "Books & Cats" design, I ventured downstairs.. Flipping the 'Open' sign with more flair than necessary, I stepped into my role as the bookstore's guardian, determined not to let a little (okay, a lot) of mystery and danger disrupt the calm rhythm of book browsing and caffeine consumption.

As I straightened stacks and woke up the cash register, my thoughts danced around the events of last night. "An unsigned note, a murder, a mysterious symbol, and us—caught in the middle. Sounds like the start of a bad detective novel, doesn't it, Jazz?" I mused aloud, earning a nonchalant meow in response. Even though things were tense, opening the store felt normal with all the adventure stories floating around.

"Alright, team," I said, addressing the empty aisles with a smirk. "Let's solve a mystery. But first, coffee." I looked at the mug I'd brought downstairs from my loft and amended my statement. "Well, *more* coffee. And maybe a scone. Priorities, after all." Munching on one of Evie's heavenly blueberry scones, I couldn't help but think I deserved it after the surprise visitor last night. I looked up to see Lottie stroll into the store with my mom, Margie, right behind her.

I did a double-take. "Mom, what are you doing here so early?"

My mother was like the Energizer Bunny, bouncing from shelf to shelf with boundless energy. "Honey, I'm here to pick a new book for the book club this month," she said, her eyes efficiently scanning the shelves. "Something thrilling, perhaps, to match the excitement around town." She practically floated on a puff of air, her fingers dancing over the spines of books, never staying still for more than a moment.

"What about 'The Mystery of the Missing Scones'?" proposed Lottie, taking the chance to tease. "Given our track record, it's bound to be a hit."

I chuckled. "Only if it's got a subplot about a relentless book club determined to solve the case through rigorous taste testing."

The banter continued between Lottie and my mother, until Margie, her attention momentarily drifting from the task at hand, leaned in with a tidbit of news. "Did you know," she began, her voice lowering as if to share a secret. "That Miranda and Professor Emerson had quite the public spat at the last community meeting? Over the Poetry Under the Stars event, of all things. Talk about professional jealousy."

I stopped, scone in hand. "Really? I hadn't heard," I replied, my brain already racing with the implications. An argument between Miranda Clarke, the town's historian, and Professor Emerson hinted at some serious underlying issues. Could this have been a motive for...?

Lottie, noticing my sudden interest, leaned in. "Well, butter my biscuits and call me a muffin! Miranda was here the night of the lecture, too, trying to shut down the event. Do you think..." she said, barely whispering.

Our eyes locked, both of us contemplating the gravity of her suggestion. The possibility Miranda might be connected to Professor Emerson's death in such a direct way hadn't fully formed in my mind until now. "Could she really have had something to do with it?" I whispered back, the question hanging in the air like a cloud. It was one thing to know about their public disagreements, but the notion it could have escalated to something else? It was just mind-boggling.

Lottie's expression mirrored my concern, a mix of disbelief and dawning apprehension. "I mean, it's possible, isn't it?"

"But why?" I asked out loud, more to myself than to Lottie. "What was so threatening about what the Professor had to say that night?"

Lottie shrugged. "I don't know, Piper. But it sounds like we have a lot more digging to do."

"I'll look into it," I declared, more to solidify my resolve than anything. "If Miranda had something to do with the Professor's death, I need to find out why." I mulled this over, a piece of the puzzle clicking into place.

Completely caught up in mind-blowing revelations, I looked at my mom, who seemed clueless about how important our conversation was. Margie was totally caught up in choosing the perfect book for her club.

"Thanks, Mom," I said, the words slipping out with a mixture of gratitude and irony. She might not have been privy to the full scope of our discussion, but in her own way, Margie had provided a crucial clue.

Margie beamed, pleased to help, blissfully unaware of the gears turning in my head. "Anytime, dear. Now, let's find that book. Something with a mystery, perhaps? Seems fitting, given the circumstances."

As we dove into the sea of titles Books and Brew offered, I pondered the deeper mystery at hand. With each new piece of information, the web of intrigue around Professor Emerson's death grew more tangled, but I was determined to unravel it. First, though, I needed to finish my scone. After all, priorities.

After my mother floated out of Books and Brew, I pulled out my phone to text Zoe.

Got a lead, I typed quickly. *Miranda and the prof had a spat before his lecture. Think it's worth digging into. Going to the station to see if I can get info from Ruby on the poison.*

I didn't wait for a response, already grabbing my purse and heading out the door, Lottie taking over for me in my absence as usual. The police station wasn't far, but with every step, my mind raced with possibilities. What was the nature of the spat? How deep did the conflict go? And most importantly, could it be the motive we were missing?

The police station was quiet, a stark contrast to the bustling energy of festival continuing downtown. I didn't want Luke to catch me snooping, so I glanced around for him. I felt relieved when I saw he wasn't around, probably out doing cop stuff or working in his office.

"Ruby," I greeted, keeping my voice low as I approached. "Got a minute?"

Ruby looked up, a knowing twinkle in her eye. "For you, always. What's up?"

I got closer, making sure no one could overhear us. "Did they get the results on the poison test?" I whispered with a deep-seated need for answers.

With a discreet glance around, Ruby leaned in to match my conspiratorial stance. "Sure did," she whispered back, her voice filled with both worry and intrigue. "The poison was rare, not something you'd find just anywhere. It's for someone who knows really knows their stuff."

"Luke's been on edge lately," she confided, her voice lowered even further, a note of caution threading through as she glanced around once more. "There's a bit of tension tied to how the investigation's progressing. It's put him in a terse mood more often than not."

"You mean he's not always so cranky?" I teased, trying to lighten the mood.

Ruby cracked a small smile, appreciating the attempt. "Believe it or not, he's usually more...let's say, composed. But the disagreements on how to handle certain aspects have really gotten to him. He's convinced there's more to the story, more avenues to explore, but he's hitting resistance." She bit her lower lip, as if considering how much gossip to dish. "His divorce was also just finalized, so that's throwing his mood off, too."

Her words painted a picture of Luke I hadn't considered before—a dedicated officer passionate about justice, now tangled in the frustrations of procedural disagreements. I didn't know he was married. Scratch him off my potential dates list. I didn't have anyone who recently ended a long-term relationship on my radar, and didn't relish being a rebound date.

"So, he thinks we're missing something important?" I prodded, curious about Luke's intuition.

"Exactly." Ruby nodded, her expression serious again. "He's been pushing to follow up on every lead, to look into all angles, no matter how unlikely they might seem. It's causing a bit of a divide within the team. Some think it's a waste of resources, but Luke - he just wants to make sure nothing gets overlooked."

"What suspects does Luke have so far? Who's he focusing on?"

Ruby checked to make sure no one was listening. "He's been super secretive, even with us at the station," she said, showing a hint of annoyance and admiration for Luke's silence. "But from the bits and pieces I've picked up, he's not ruling anyone out. Charlie Alderton and Miranda Clarke are definitely on his radar, especially with their known conflicts with the professor."

The names weren't a surprise, but hearing Luke was also considering them reaffirmed my own suspicions and the direction of our investigation. "He's thorough, I'll give him that," I murmured, a plan beginning to take shape in my mind.

"He is," Ruby agreed, a hint of pride in her voice. "And despite the pushback, he's determined to follow through on every lead, no matter where it takes him. Just...be careful, Piper. Whoever did this...they're not playing around."

I dipped out of the police station and went straight to Zoe's shop. I only had to take a short walk through the downtown area, and I wanted to give her the lowdown on what happened last night and Ruby's key info.

Stepping into Palette Whispers, I heard the jingle I knew so well, like the soundtrack to our newest adventure. Zoe was totally in her zone, surrounded by a bunch of art supplies and half-done master-pieces.

I walked in, surrounded by all these amazing colors and creativity. "You'll never believe who just got promoted to detective extraordinaire in Maplebrook."

Zoe glanced up with a smirk. "Sherlock Holmes or Nancy Drew? No, wait—Piper Page, of course. Lay it on me."

I told the story of the mysterious book, hoping for a big reaction, but Zoe was mostly just pumped. "Creepy messages in mystery novels? That's our jam, isn't it?" she asked, her eyes sparkling with intrigue.

"And if you think that's juicy..." I continued, diving into the details Ruby had reluctantly shared—about the poison and the internal squabbles plaguing the police department.

"Internal drama? Sounds like our police department's version of a soap opera. And Luke's the star? I'd watch that." Then Zoe leaned in. "You won't believe who popped in earlier—Derek from Vintage Vinyl," she whispered the juicy tidbit she'd heard this morning. "He was practically spilling the tea on Miranda and Emerson. According to Derek, our esteemed local historian was fuming more than his old espresso machine. Professor Emerson had been openly questioning the authenticity of documents she'd authenticated. Can you imagine being in her shoes? I'd probably—"

"Throw a historic tantrum?" I finished for her, both of us acknowledging the gravity behind the laughter.

"Exactly," Zoe said, her laughter fading into a more serious contemplation. "But seriously, if Miranda felt cornered, threatened even, who knows what lengths she'd go to protect her legacy?"

I nodded, my mind racing. "Just what I was thinking. I might do some snooping around. How about we have a little chat with Miranda? I'm planning on stopping by the Historical Museum later to see what else I can discover."

Zoe's look went from intrigued to determined. "Count me in. This is getting too interesting to sit out. Plus, I've got a few artful questions of my own for our local historian."

Chapter Seven

♥

Lottie and I worked all afternoon at Books and Brew, scrambling to prepare for the literary cafe crawl in the evening. Part of the festival, the event promised an enchanting journey through various cafes, each hosting readings and discussions on different literary themes. Books and Brew was the place to be, with its cozy vibe and shelves packed with stories, creating the perfect setting to explore the wonders of literature.

As I grabbed one of the frosted sugar cookies Evie had generously supplied from The Sugar Whisk, I couldn't resist taking a large, satisfying bite.

Lottie eyed the cookie with mock severity. "Piper, if you eat all the evidence of Evie's hard work before the guests arrive, we'll have a new mystery on our hands."

I chuckled, crumbs betraying my guilty pleasure. "*The Mystery of the Vanishing Cookies*", I declared, adopting an exaggerated tone of intrigue. "A tale of temptation and betrayal, where the prime suspect has an insatiable sweet tooth."

Lottie shook her head, laughing. "Just make sure you leave some clues for our guests to enjoy. We wouldn't want to disappoint the literary crowd with a shortage of sweets."

Zoe suddenly burst in, right on cue. "Am I interrupting a crucial case briefing, or can a fellow sleuth join the investigation?"

"The more, the merrier," I replied, offering her a cookie as evidence. "Just be warned, the stakes are high, and the sweets are disappearing fast."

Just as Zoe was about to answer, another voice broke the playful mood. "If you're looking for a warning, here's a better one: let the police handle the investigation, Piper."

We all jumped as Luke appeared in the doorway, looking serious. He clearly found out about our amateur detective work and was not happy.

Zoe, not bothered at all, responded to his seriousness with her usual lightheartedness. "Come on, Luke. Lighten up! We're just doing our part. This is our town, too, you know."

I nodded in agreement, unable to resist teasing him a little. "Besides, someone has to keep the literary spirit alive, even amid mystery. We're practically honorary detectives at this point."

Luke's frown got deeper, but he had a hard time hiding his amusement. Despite his objections, he understood our attachment to Maplebrook and our desire to protect it.

" 'Honorary detectives,'" Luke grumbled, sarcastically emphasizing the title. "Just be careful, okay? This isn't a game."

"We get it," I chimed in, catching the hint of worry tucked away under his tough cop facade. "But you can't fault us for having a soft spot for our little town. In addition, someone killed the Professor in my store. That feels personal."

He agreed, his stance softening just a fraction, enough to let the light of his underlying concern shine through. "But if I even get one whiff that you're stepping into anything dangerous, it ends right there, got it?"

I decided to keep quiet about the strange book which mysteriously popped up outside Books and Brew last night. Somehow, I knew if Luke were clued in, he'd draw a firm line in the sand then and there. "Got it." I rolled my eyes with a theatrical sigh for added effect.

"Sure, Luke, we'll just stick to dangerous levels of caffeine and possibly risky sugar intakes from all these cookies," Zoe chimed in, her grin betraying her mock solemnity. "Those are the kind of dangers we're trained to handle."

As Luke made his exit, presumably to save the town from more dire threats than two amateur detectives, Zoe and I couldn't help but let out a giggle.

"Watch out, Zoe, his 'cop radar' is tuned to our frequency now. Next thing you know, he'll be issuing citations for excessive snooping," I said, still amused by the whole interaction.

Zoe snorted, playfully adopting a stance of mock vigilance. "In that case, I'll start practicing my 'innocent bystander' face. Or maybe we need a secret handshake for our undercover operations."

We laughed and said goodbye to Lottie, who couldn't hide her amusement. "Keep the fort down, Lottie, and save some cookies for us."

We went to the Historical Museum, hoping to find Miranda and figure out what was going on. Upon arrival, however, Miranda was conspicuously absent. Instead, we were greeted by Dean Foster, the museum's curator, who was as big a deal as the artifacts he protected.

I casually struck up a chat with Dean, keeping my detective hat well-hidden under a veil of genuine interest. "The way you animate Maplebrook's past is nothing short of magical. Working with Professor Emerson must have been like collaborating with a time-traveler, huh?"

The curator, always ready to champion his role as Maplebrook's unofficial timekeeper, couldn't hide his enthusiasm. "Professor Emerson brought more than his fair share of excitement to our exhibits," he shared. "Let's just say his theories occasionally caused a bit of a stir in our usually-calm historical waters."

I was on the lookout for any interesting clues to connect to our mystery, so I prodded the conversation along. "History's like a live show, always adding new acts. I bet the Professor's latest discoveries were like dropping a plot twist in the season finale. Stirred up some lively debates, I'd guess."

At the mention of Professor Emerson's contentious findings, Dean's warm demeanor took on a slight edge, though he maintained his composure. "History does love a good debate. Professor Emerson certainly had his opinions. But here, we try to paint a picture that fits the whole gallery, not just one piece," he deflected, diplomatically toeing the line between open and guarded.

Zoe, ever the source of levity, jumped in with a grin. "Sounds like the Professor was more blockbuster action, while the museum prefers a classic drama. Makes for an interesting mix at the concession stand, doesn't it?"

Dean laughed, caught off-guard by Zoe's analogy. "Indeed, we've got all genres represented. And trust me, keeping harmony in the historical narrative? It's more art than science."

"Speaking of art and science, you're coming to the Poetry Under the Stars event later this week, right?" asked Zoe, always ready to transition from sleuth to socialite, smoothly changed the subject. "It's going to be the blockbuster of Maplebrook's social season."

I nodded in agreement. "It'd be great to see you there. And thanks for sharing your time—and your insights—with us. Always enlightening to dive into Maplebrook's stories with someone as knowledge-able as you."

Dean, visibly pleased by the invitation and our appreciation, assured us with a warm smile. "I wouldn't miss it. And you're always welcome here. History's not just about the past; it's about sharing stories with the future."

With that, Zoe and I thanked him once more and made our way out of the museum.

"That was enlightening, but no Miranda," I remarked, feeling a mix of curiosity and frustration.

Zoe, ever the optimist, shrugged. "Every clue helps, right? Plus, Dean was a goldmine, even if he didn't mean to be."

As we strolled back to Books and Brew, getting ready for the evening's literary cafe crawl, it hit me – I remembered something else Ruby had told me. "Charlie Alderton is another name that popped up on Luke's radar," I said, turning to Zoe. "And Sophie wrote that article about the Alderton family the other day. Might be worth looking into, given the... colorful history there."

Zoe nodded. "Ah, the Alderton legacy. Drama, history, and a touch of scandal. Classic Maplebrook cocktail," she mused, the gears in her head visibly turning. "Think he'll be at the cafe crawl tonight?"

I mulled over Zoe's question, rubbing my chin. "The Alderton legacy is like Maplebrook's own version of a serial, isn't it? Charlie showing up tonight is anyone's guess. But since he's been trying to sort things out, the cafe crawl could be just what he needs. Public, lots of ears, and amidst the very essence of storytelling." I paused, a smirk playing on my lips. "If he makes an appearance, it'll be the highlight of the evening, no doubt. Drama aside, it's an opportunity too good for someone in his shoes to pass up. I say we keep our eyes peeled and our notebooks ready."

As Zoe and I made our way back to Books and Brew, we passed by Cuppa Joe's, a cornerstone in the Maplebrook community and the source of some of the best coffee served at my bookstore café. Joe Harrison, the shop's affable owner, always had a knack for creating a welcoming space with his eclectic decor and exceptional java. I'd been buying his beans for Books and Brew for years, valuing not just the quality but also the connection it fostered within our small community.

When I saw Joe setting up some new chairs outside, I just had to stop for a quick chat. I waved as we approached. "How's everything at the coffee kingdom?"

Joe looked up, grinning from ear to ear. "Great to see you two. Just getting ready for the day's rush. What can I do for you? More of our special blend for Books and Brew?"

I loved Joe's warm reception. "We'll never run the risk of a coffee drought, thanks to you. But we were meandering through town, soaking up the latest. Anything juicy floating around the gossip grapevine?"

Joe leaned back, a twinkle of amusement in his eyes. "Maplebrook never disappoints on that front," he started, wiping his hands on a cloth. "Mrs. Patterson's cat, Whiskers, has apparently taken up residence at the library. Refuses to leave. And the Jenkins twins have somehow managed to dye the fountain water blue—again."

Zoe burst out laughing. "Classic Jenkins move. But honestly, Whiskers might just be the most well-read cat in history by now."

As our laughter subsided, Joe shifted, his tone taking on a hint of intrigue. "On a more heated note, Charlie Alderton was here earlier, all riled up. He's on a mission to correct some stories about his family's history. Seems there's been quite a bit of chatter he's not too pleased about. Wants to set the record straight, he says."

I exchanged a glance with Zoe, both of us noting the information. "Charlie's always been passionate about his family's legacy."

"Sure has," Joe agreed, nodding. "Anyway, let me know when you need more coffee. Always happy to keep Books and Brew caffeinated."

"Will do, Joe. Thanks for the chat," I said as we waved goodbye and continued on our way.

His casual mention of Charlie's visit added an interesting angle. As Zoe and I walked back to Books and Brew, we mulled over the new info. Charlie's determination to defend his family's reputation was definitely something we had to consider. With the literary cafe crawl on the horizon, our minds were abuzz with not just the anticipation of the event, but also the mysteries slowly unraveling in Maplebrook.

Chapter Eight

♥

Fresh from our enlightening visit to Cuppa Joe's, Zoe and I returned to the bookstore, just in time for the literary cafe crawl. The store was alive with excitement, smelling of books and freshly-brewed coffee. The event was all about exploring literature. Local authors read fiction, non-fiction, and poetry at different spots downtown in Maplebrook.

Martin Fields, known for his epic historical fiction, was there, along with Sarah Jennings, who'd just won a ton of praise for her modern poetry. But it was the announcement of Julia Hart's attendance which had Lottie practically bouncing on her heels with excitement. Julia, a bestselling romance author, was Lottie's favorite, and her presence at Books and Brew was something Lottie had been looking forward to for weeks.

"I can't believe Julia Hart is going to be here, in our little bookstore!" Lottie exclaimed as she helped set up chairs and arrange the space for the evening's guests. "I've read all her books at least twice. Do you think she'll sign my copies?"

Lottie's enthusiasm made me smile, it was contagious. "I'm sure she'd be delighted. Just make sure you save some of that energy for helping us host tonight." I earned an excited nod from her as she dashed off to ensure everything was perfect for Julia's arrival.

As I busied myself behind the counter, ensuring every detail was in place for the evening, my hand brushed against something unexpected—a sealed envelope tucked under a stack of event flyers. "Really, what is this? Mystery clue delivery day?" I muttered to myself, half-amused, half-bewildered by the seemingly endless stream of cryptic messages finding their way to me. "At this rate, I might as well start a lost and found for anonymous tips."

With a mix of resignation and curiosity, I carefully tucked the envelope in my apron pocket. I'd give it a closer look when I wasn't so swamped. The event was starting, and we were quickly filling with the buzz of conversation and the soft rustling of pages as patrons settled into their seats, eagerly expecting the night's literary offerings.

The cafe crawl was in full swing, with each author's reading captivating the audience, weaving a tapestry of narratives which spanned genres and eras. It was during a poignant moment in Sarah Jennings' poetry reading when I felt the envelope's weight in my pocket, a silent reminder of the mystery which lay sealed within.

Once the clapping died down and people started chatting over coffee and cake, I saw my opportunity. I snagged a quiet corner at Books and Brew and motioned for Zoe to join me, giving her a look of urgency. "Look what I found," I whispered, barely containing the mix of excitement and nervousness the sealed envelope had instigated.

Together, we hunched over the letter, our heads close, as I carefully broke the seal, my fingers trembling with the anticipation of what secrets it might unveil. The letter was all worn and delicate, but the words on it were crystal clear—a detailed story of a secret meetup between Charlie Alderton and Professor Emerson. Phrases like "urgent discussion" and "necessary revelations" jumped out at me, hinting at a depth to their relationship which went beyond simple acquaintance. Mention of a contested discovery by Professor Emerson suggested a motive tangled in academic rivalry and personal pride, painting a picture of a partnership strained by secrets and, ultimately, tragedy.

"This could be huge," Zoe murmured, her voice a mix of awe and concern.

I nodded, feeling the weight of the discovery on our shoulders. "We need to document this," I said, echoing the seriousness of our find.

"Let's take a photo," suggested Zoe, quick to think on her feet. "Just in case we have to pass it on to Luke later."

Carefully, Zoe held the letter steady as I snapped a picture with my phone, ensuring we had a digital copy of a crucial piece of evidence. As Zoe and I huddled over the letter, deciphering its contents with a growing sense of urgency, we heard the excited patter of footsteps approaching.

Lottie bounded over, her enthusiasm nearly palpable, a sharp contrast to the gravity of our discovery. "Guess what? Julia Hart signed my copy of *Love in Lavender Fields*! Look!" Lottie gushed, thrusting the book in front of us, her eyes sparkling with delight. The book's cover, featuring a sweeping landscape of purple hues, seemed to dance under the bookstore's warm lighting.

"That's amazing, Lottie!" I said, my voice laced with genuine happiness for her despite the tension of the moment. "Did she give you any tips on how to write the perfect love scene?"

"Yeah, Lottie, do share," Zoe, ever the quick-witted one, chimed in with a smirk. "We could use a bit of romance to lighten up our mystery thriller life here."

Lottie, oblivious to the sarcasm, nodded enthusiastically. "She said it's all about the build-up and the tension—you know, like the suspense in your...what are you two doing, anyway?" Her gaze finally landed on the letter between us, her curiosity piqued.

"Just solving a mystery, Lottie-style," Zoe quipped, tucking her phone away after capturing the letter. "But instead of love letters, we get cryptic notes. Less romance, more intrigue. We'll show you later."

As Lottie hurried off to finish her closing duties, still buzzing from Julia Hart's visit, Sophie's sharp voice abruptly interrupted the friendly atmosphere. The local reporter had a way of popping up when I least expected—or wanted—her to.

"Piper, can we discuss tonight's event?" Sophie's voice, though polite on the surface, carried an undercurrent of relentless curiosity. "After the murder the other evening, were you hesitant to host again? Has it affected your sales?"

Her line of questioning made me uncomfortable, as if she was scrutinizing me. It wasn't only about the event or the bookstore, it felt like an indictment of my decision to keep the doors of Books and Brew open, to foster a sense of normalcy and safety in a community rocked by uncertainty. "The community should feel safe in their local bookstore," I replied, my voice firm, tinged with a protective edge. "What happened was tragic, but it shouldn't cast a shadow over Books and Brew or the events we host. If you're looking for a story, maybe you should focus on the actual issue—finding Professor Emerson's killer, not whether it's affecting my bottom line."

Sophie looked a little shocked at how straightforward I was. It was obvious she didn't expect me to question her story. "I see," she said after a moment, her pen pausing over her notepad. "So, you believe the community should continue to come together, not let this... isolate them?"

"Absolutely," I affirmed, softening slightly but standing my ground. "Books and Brew is more than just a bookstore. It's a place where people can connect, share stories, and find comfort in words. That's more important now than ever."

Sophie nodded, her expression unreadable as she jotted down a few last notes. "Thank you for your time, Piper. I'll include your perspective in my piece."

As she walked away, I let out a slow breath, feeling a mix of frustration and relief. The encounter was totally unexpected, reminding us the murder had a big impact on our entire community. But it also reminded me how strong Maplebrook was and how important the bookstore was to it.

I smiled weakly at Zoe, who had been watching with a mix of support and caution. "Well, that was fun," I said, the sarcasm not quite masking my lingering irritation.

Zoe's laughter still echoed softly in the air, a testament to our ability to find lightness even in the most tangled situations. "You handled that like a pro. Sophie's tough, but she's got nothing on you," she affirmed, her admiration clear.

Buoyed by Zoe's words, I was about to tuck the letter back into my bag for safekeeping when the atmosphere shifted palpably. An ominous presence pierced the warm buzz of the event, and both Zoe and I felt the change instantly. As we turned around, we saw a figure come out of nowhere, and it was staring right where I was about to put the letter. Creepy.

"I think you've got something that doesn't belong to you," the man said, his voice smooth yet edged with a chill that ran down my spine. He was dressed in dark, nondescript clothing, with a hood pulled low over his face and gloves covering his hands—making it impossible to identify him.

I tightened my grip on the paper, my shock quickly turning into defiance. "Actually, this was left for me. It's very much my business," I retorted, my voice steady even as my heart thundered against my ribs.

He stepped closer, his intent clear in his narrowed gaze. "I'm afraid you're mistaken. Hand it over, and we can all walk away from this little misunderstanding," he pressed, the threat in his tone unmistakable.

Zoe, usually the one to lighten the mood, stepped forward, her demeanor shifting to one of protection. "I don't think so," she challenged, standing firmly by my side. "We don't even know who you are."

The curious crowd, drawn towards the commotion, suddenly interrupted our standoff. In the moment of distraction, the man lunged for the letter, snatching it away. The commotion got the crowd curious.

As he disappeared into the sea of people, Zoe and I found ourselves in the echoing silence of our loss. The room seemed to spin, the vibrant chatter of the guests now a distant hum, as I tried to process what had just happened.

"We have to get it back," I said, determination welling up inside me. "That letter could be the key to everything."

When the bookstore finally grew quiet, Zoe and I leaned against the counter, the weight of the evening's events settling around us like a heavy cloak. Jazz sauntered over, giving us a once-over with his green eyes. I picked him up, and right away, he started purring, which was a slight comfort in the middle of all the chaos.

"He always knows when things are off, doesn't he?" I murmured, giving Jazz a little scratch on the head. His purring intensified, as if to agree or perhaps just to offer his own kind of support.

Zoe chuckled softly, watching us. "If only he could talk, huh? Imagine the secrets he could spill. Though, knowing Jazz, he'd probably just complain about the lack of tuna treats around here."

I couldn't help but smile, even though I was a mess inside. "Or he'd blackmail us into endless belly rubs. He's got that devious look about him."

Jazz, pleased with being the center of attention, nuzzled against my hand.

I let out a sigh, feeling the weight of responsibility on me. "Let's look at the photo we took. Maybe there's something we missed." Pulling out my phone, I opened the image of the letter we'd captured before it was snatched from us. Zoe leaned in, her keen eyes scanning the digital copy.

The clue we discovered in the letter's photo was a small, hand-drawn map sketched in the margin—a detail so minute and seemingly inconsequential, it had gone unnoticed during our initial scrutiny. The map, though crude, clearly highlighted a specific area on the outskirts of Maplebrook, marked with an X. Just beside it, almost as an afterthought, were the initials "R.E."—undoubtedly referring to Robert Emerson.

The minor note, kind of hidden among the more important stuff in the letter, now screamed its significance. Professor Emerson had taken care to include a physical location, a tangible piece of the puzzle hidden within what appeared to be an ordinary correspondence.

"This could be exactly what Professor Emerson was killed for. If we can find this place..." Zoe's voice trailed off, the implications of our discovery hanging heavily between us.

The significance of the discovery was not lost on me. "It might prove Emerson was right all along. And it could lead us straight to the murderer."

Suddenly, there was a loud pounding on the store's door. The sound was angry, and it echoed throughout the quiet room. I could see Luke's silhouette through the glass, and he looked mad. Really mad.

Zoe looked at me with a smirk, but I could tell she was worried. "Looks like we're in for it now," she half-joked, her voice low.

I hesitantly opened the door, preparing for the storm.

Luke ran in, his anger filling the room, and his eyes locked onto mine with a powerful intensity. "Piper," he started, his tone a volatile mix of anger and deep concern, amplified by what he'd heard about the evening's events. "Do you realize how reckless you're being? This isn't some game of detective you're playing—you're meddling in affairs that could put you in real danger."

His accusation hit me like a cold splash of reality, yet it only fortified my resolve rather than dampened it. "We're not playing at anything," I shot back, my frustration rising to match his. "We're trying to uncover the truth, to bring some closure for our community. And if you heard about tonight, then you should know that we're onto something significant."

Luke was unyielding, his duty as an officer clear in his rigid stance. "Leave it to the police, Piper. We're equipped to handle this. You and Zoe need to step back before you get yourselves hurt—or worse."

Zoe and I exchanged a look, silently agreeing as we dealt with Luke's stubbornness. Both of us let out a synchronized huff, our arms folding defensively across our chests, a clear sign we weren't backing down. Luke's worry for our safety, though rooted in genuine concern, couldn't dampen our resolve. Right at that moment, Jazz plopped down in the middle of us, completely unaware of the tension. He rolled onto his side, silently begging for belly rubs, his way of negotiating amidst all the conflict.

"Finally, someone who knows how to compromise," I joked, giving Jazz a sideways glance and a half-smile. I decided I wasn't quite ready to give the detective our picture of the mysterious letter yet.

Chapter Nine

♥

Zoe and I were squinting at the photo of the letter on my phone in the creepy, lamp-lit back room of Books and Brew. Trying to decipher the details on the small screen was like reading the fine print in a contract without my glasses—possible, but I might adopt a llama without realizing it. Just when we were in the middle of being serious detectives, Jazz came over for some love.

"Look at this part, Zoe," I pointed to the section of the photo where "Thornhill's Grove" was barely legible. "Isn't that the original founding spot for Maplebrook? Maybe Professor Emerson found something big there—big enough to shake up what Miranda Clarke has been preaching about Maplebrook's history."

Zoe's eyes widened. "You're right. Thornhill's Grove is where Jonathan Maplebrook's wife, Eliza, is buried. That place has always been significant."

I nodded, feeling a surge of determination. "If that's true, it could explain why someone would go to such lengths to keep it a secret. Preserving the historical site or revealing some hidden truth—either way, it's a huge deal. We need to check it out for ourselves. Whatever it is, we'll find it."

"Agreed," Zoe said. "First thing tomorrow, we head to Thornhill's Grove. Let's see what Professor Emerson uncovered."

Jazz decided to steal the spotlight during our brainstorming session by leaping onto the table like a sumo wrestler, nearly sending my phone flying. "Jazz, buddy, this isn't the time to audition for 'Cats on Ice,'" I said, easing him back to the floor.

"We should really talk to Miranda about this...gently," I suggested, imagining the confrontation. "Maybe without mentioning we think she's part of a historical cover-up conspiracy."

"And maybe without Jazz. I love him, but he's not cut out for secret missions," Zoe said, looking down at Jazz who was grooming himself, totally unfazed by our plans.

"And Luke," Zoe continued, her smile fading a bit. "He's going to want to wrap us in bubble wrap and store us in a safe if he finds out we're going after Miranda with questions about secret groves and founding family feuds."

I couldn't help but laugh, even though I was worried about how Luke would react. "Let's worry about bubble wrap later. For now, we've got some history to uncover. And maybe keep Jazz out of the loop—he's liable to spill the beans for a can of tuna."

As Jazz tried to scale the bookshelf in search of an imaginary foe, we prepared ourselves to uncover the Thornhill's Grove mystery and Miranda's juicy secrets.

"Lottie, would you mind being captain of the ship for a while?" I asked, nodding towards the front of the store where Lottie was meticulously organizing a display of new arrivals, her excitement over meeting Julia Hart still visible in her animated movements.

The older woman looked up, playfully saluting. "Sure thing, Captain! The treasure is safe with me, no worries. Or until you come back," she said with a grin, clearly enjoying her temporary promotion.

With Lottie now in charge of Books and Brew, Zoe and I set off to the Maplebrook Historical Museum. It was the perfect place to casually run into Miranda Clarke and pretend to be interested in working together.

Stepping into the museum felt like going back in time. As we navigated through exhibits of sepia-toned photographs and artifacts, the weight of the town's past pressed in around us. It didn't take long before we spotted Miranda, completely absorbed in an exhibit about the founding families.

I approached with a smile I hoped appeared genuine and not at all like we were subtly planning on interrogating her. "We were just talking about how amazing it would be to bring some of this history into Zoe's art store. Perhaps an exhibit inspired by Professor Emerson's work?"

Miranda acted cool, just raised her eyebrow a bit when she saw us. "Professor Emerson's research? His theories were...divisive, to say the least," she responded, her tone neutral but her eyes wary.

Zoe, ever the diplomat, stepped in. "But controversy can spark interest, right? Especially something as intriguing as his work on Thornhill's Grove." Her casual mention of the Grove cast a line, waiting to see if Miranda would bite.

The mention of Thornhill's Grove prompted a visible shift in Miranda's demeanor. A flicker of something—was it concern? Annoyance?—crossed her face before she composed herself. "Thornhill's Grove is a mere footnote in Maplebrook's vast history," she replied coolly. "Hardly worth the sensationalism some have attributed to it."

Miranda tried to downplay Thornhill's Grove, but I remembered how strongly she objected to Professor Emerson's lecture at Books and Brew. The memory sparked a playful, yet pointed, retort. "Speaking of sensationalism," I said, a half-smile dancing on my lips. "You seemed quite passionate about halting Professor Emerson's lecture the other night. For something that was just a 'footnote,' it must have really ruffled your feathers, huh?"

Miranda's poker face slipped just a little, revealing a crack in her act. "That was a matter of historical accuracy," she responded, a hint of defensiveness creeping into her voice. "Professor Emerson's theories, while interesting, were speculative at best. Letting them be presented as fact would have been irresponsible."

Zoe, seizing the moment, leaned in a tad. "Sounds like the kind of speculation that keeps people talking, though. And here we are, still discussing it."

Miranda gave us a look, like she was reevaluating us as more than just bookstore owners, but as people who could challenge her. "As I was saying, Maplebrook has a fascinating history. It's important that we present it responsibly."

After we wrapped up our conversation and left the museum, Zoe whispered, "That was like poking a bear with a very historical stick."

Back at Books and Brew, we shared our adventure with Lottie, who was both amused and intrigued by our encounter with Miranda. "Alright, what's the game plan now? Going to dig up the whole grove ourselves?" Her eyes twinkled with excitement and a hint of mischief.

"Maybe not tonight," I said. "But we're getting closer. Thornhill's Grove isn't just a footnote—it's the next chapter."

That afternoon, Maplebrook buzzed with anticipation for Poetry Under the Stars, a standout event at the Pages and Prose Festival. In the bustling town square, the event would come alive with the captivating words of poetry readings and the vibrant atmosphere of open-mic sessions. Local and guest poets would share their verses with an appreciative audience.

That afternoon, when Zoe and I got downtown to lend a hand, the town square was alive with excitement. The atmosphere was lively as we occupied ourselves with the meticulous task of arranging chairs and setting up the stage, with our efforts occasionally interrupted by bursts of laughter and playful banter.

"Could you imagine us getting up there tonight?" Zoe asked as she unfurled a banner. "I'd probably end up pioneering a genre I'd call 'accidental limericks'."

Grinning, I adjusted a microphone stand. "I'm there for it. But only if I can follow up with my 'serendipitous sonnets'. We'll start a trend."

Everyone, from business owners to locals, pitched in, and the atmosphere filled with camaraderie. Charlie from The Prairie Plate was overseeing the catering setup, promising a feast as memorable as the poetry.

"Piper, Zoe," greeted Mrs. Jenkins, who ran the local flower shop, carrying a basket of floral arrangements for the stage. "How's the poetic endeavor going?"

"We're thinking of founding a society," Zoe said with a wide smile. "Membership, open?"

"Count me in," Mrs. Jenkins laughed, setting down her basket and arranging the flowers with an artist's touch.

Charlie looked up, his hands still for a moment as he registered my question. A smile creased his face, the kind of smile that comes with pride in one's work. "You mean joining the accidental poets' club?" he asked, following our banter. "I think I'll stick to what I know best. Let's just say my talents lie more in the culinary arts than the literary ones."

"Fair enough," Zoe chimed in, her voice laced with laughter. "But if you ever decide to venture into culinary poetry, you'd have a captive audience with us."

The vibe around the food setup felt cozy, like a big family gathering, with everyone excited to try Charlie's famous dishes and feel the overall excitement of the night.

Taking advantage of the momentary pause in setup activities, I steered the conversation towards a topic which had been burning at the back of my mind. "We were actually talking about Maplebrook's history earlier," I ventured, trying to sound as nonchalant as possible. "Especially Professor Emerson's interest in Thornhill's Grove. It's such a fascinating piece of local lore, don't you think?"

Charlie's demeanor shifted slightly, a subtle change which might have gone unnoticed to anyone not looking for it. He carefully placed a loaf of bread on a cutting board. "The Professor had quite the fascination with that place. Said it was key to understanding the real history of Maplebrook. I suppose he might have been onto something, but you know how it is with history—it's all about the stories we choose to tell."

Charlie's subtle shift didn't go unnoticed, so I lightened things up to keep the conversation flowing. "Speaking of stories," I began with a playful tilt of my head and a mischievous glint in my eye. "I heard you and Professor Emerson had quite the spirited debate earlier this week. Any interesting tales to share?"

For a moment, Charlie's eyes met mine, a flicker of surprise—or was it apprehension?—passing through them before he masked it with a good-natured chuckle. He busied himself with arranging the artisanal cheese platter, a task which suddenly required his full attention. "You know how it is," he finally said, his voice carrying a note of dismissiveness that was almost too casual. "Academic types like the Professor, they get passionate about their work. And sometimes, that passion spills over. We had a...let's call it a 'lively discussion' about

Maplebrook's history. But it was all in the spirit of intellectual debate, nothing more."

Zoe leaned in and added her own touch of humor. "Sounds like Maplebrook's version of a dramatic showdown. Should we expect a dramatic reenactment tonight amidst the poetry readings?"

Charlie laughed, this time more genuinely, appreciating Zoe's attempt to keep things light. "I think tonight's drama will be limited to the poetic kind," he assured us. "Though, who knows? Maplebrook always has a way of surprising us."

Charlie shared his story about the 'lively discussion' he had with the Professor when Ethan Hargrove, a well-known member of the community and one of the sponsors of the literary festival, showed up. He had perfect timing, making our casual conversation even better.

"Well, well, look who it is," I greeted Ethan with a grin, curious about why he appeared out of the blue. "We were just discussing Maplebrook's rich, and sometimes contested, history."

Ethan, always poised and ready with a word of wisdom, nodded in acknowledgment. "History is a curious thing, isn't it? Full of tales that twist and turn with the telling." He glanced at Charlie and back to us, a knowing look in his eyes. "I've heard a bit about Professor Emerson's recent endeavors. Fascinating stuff, though I had no direct involvement."

When he mentioned the Professor, I got interested and leaned in, not wanting to miss anything. "You've heard about his work on Thornhill's Grove, then?"

"Bits and pieces," Ethan admitted, his expression thoughtful. "Rumors mostly, nothing concrete. But if you're really looking to dig deeper, the town's archives might hold some clues. Thornhill's Grove has always had a bit of mystery surrounding it."

The suggestion was like a lightbulb moment. Zoe and I shared a glance, realizing how valuable Ethan's advice was. "The archives, of course!" Zoe exclaimed, her voice a mix of excitement and gratitude. "Why didn't we think of that sooner?"

Ethan smiled, pleased to have been of help. "Just remember, history has a way of revealing more than you expect. Tread carefully."

With Ethan's departure to mingle with other guests and fulfill his obligations as a sponsor, Zoe and I were presented with a fresh avenue to discover. Charlie, too, seemed intrigued by the mention of the archives, though he quickly masked his interest with a return to his catering duties.

"Looks like our investigation just got a new direction," I whispered, turning to Zoe with renewed determination. "The town's archives might just hold the key to unlocking Emerson's secrets and unraveling the mystery of Thornhill's Grove."

Zoe nodded in agreement, her level of excitement mirroring my own. "And maybe, just maybe, we'll find what Emerson was willing to risk so much for."

Chapter Ten

♥

The library's tall windows allowed the afternoon sun to gently filter in, creating beautiful patterns of light and casting long shadows which stretched across the tables adorned with an abundance of books and papers. Zoe and I were huddled in a quiet corner, going through old city council records and land deeds on the microfilm reader. Our search was methodical, driven by the fragments of a story we were desperate to piece together. That's when we stumbled upon it: a document that changed everything.

"Zoe, look at this," I whispered, my voice trembling with excitement and disbelief. Displayed on the screen was a petition supported by Miranda Clarke, promoting a significant development project right next to Thornhill's Grove. But it wasn't just any project; this development stood to gain enormously, should certain historical claims—claims Emerson was on the verge of proving—vanish into obscurity.

Zoe's eyes widened as she read over my shoulder. "This is it, Piper. It proves Miranda had a motive. If Professor Emerson's research went public--"

"She's in danger of losing everything," I said, the weight of our discovery sinking in. There was no denying it now. Miranda wasn't just a historian interested in preserving Maplebrook's past; she was actively shaping it to her advantage.

We sat in silence for a moment. "We should just confront her," I said, feeling terrified but knowing we had no other choice. "Tonight, at the Poetry Under the Stars event. It's the perfect opportunity."

When we returned to Books and Brew, the café buzzed with lively chatter, the murmurs of the afternoon clientele harmonizing with the delightful clinks of coffee cups, filling my heart with pure delight. Lottie was all ears as we spilled the beans about our latest detective escapade.

"Let me get this straight," Lottie said, a playful smirk dancing on her lips. "You two are turning into Maplebrook's very own Holmes and Watson? Should I expect to be serving mystery-themed coffee next?"

Zoe laughed, her notes rustling as she flipped through them. "Only if you can brew a blend that tastes like intrigue and whispered secrets."

I grinned, riding their humor wave. "And a dash of danger. We're thinking about confronting Miranda tonight. Got any tips on how to do that without turning it into a dramatic showdown?"

Lottie paused, and her usual mischievous glint appeared in her eyes. "Simple. Start with casual chitchat. People can't resist spilling their secrets if you talk about the weather long enough. It's the Maplebrook way."

"Brilliant," Zoe said. "We'll disarm her with small talk about the chance of rain. She won't see it coming."

As we finalized our plan, I realized we couldn't go through with it without informing Luke. I pulled out my phone and dialed his number, waiting as it rang.

"Piper?" Luke answered, a hint of surprise in his voice. "What's up?"

"Hey," I began, trying to keep my voice steady. "We've come up with a plan to talk to Miranda. We think she might open up to us in a way she wouldn't with the police. We're going to approach her tonight."

There was a pause on the other end, followed by a sigh. "I've told you all before, I don't want you involving yourselves in the investigation. It's dangerous."

"I know," I said earnestly, "but we genuinely want to help. We can get Miranda to talk. We'll be careful, I promise."

He was silent for a moment, and I could practically hear him weighing his options. "Alright, fine," he relented, "but only on one condition. You both wear wires when you speak to Miranda. That way, if anything goes wrong, I'll know immediately and can step in."

I glanced at Zoe, who nodded in agreement. "Deal," I said. "We'll wear the wires."

"I'll drop them off at Books and Brew in ten minutes," Luke said, his tone firm. "And remember, if things start to go south, get out of there immediately."

"Got it. Thanks," I replied, feeling a mix of relief and apprehension.

True to his word, Luke arrived shortly after with two small devices. "These are pretty discreet," he explained, handing them to us. "Just clip them under your clothes. And stay safe."

With a plan that was a blend of careful strategy and spontaneous improvisation, Zoe and I readied ourselves to depart, our spirits lifted by the camaraderie and lighthearted banter of our close-knit group. The evening promised poetry under the stars, but for us, it held the promise of answers—answers we were more determined than ever to uncover, armed with our wits, our friends' support, and maybe, just maybe, a bit of small talk about the weather.

As the day folded into the cooler hues of the evening, Lottie and I closed Books and Brew early. We were filled with anticipation as we locked up the café, the warmth of the day still present. The town square, usually a canvas of mundane daily activities, had transformed into a literary oasis under the open sky, awaiting the night's Poetry Under the Stars event.

The square was buzzing with a communal energy, the kind that only Maplebrook could bring on nights like these. String lights criss-crossed above, casting a soft glow which made the cobblestones underfoot seem to shimmer. Small groups of chairs formed a semi-circle around a modest wooden stage, which had a vintage microphone adorning its surface, waiting for the voices of the night's poets.

As Lottie and I walked around, we said hi to people we knew, feeling the warmth of our community. My mother, Margie, flanked by Ruby, waved enthusiastically from where they stood near the refreshment table, a spread generously donated by local businesses.

My mother beamed. "Doesn't everything look great?" she asked as her eyes scanned the scene with evident pride. "I just love seeing Maplebrook come together like this."

As she talked, her eyes briefly wandered to Luke, who was chatting with locals and effortlessly commanding the spotlight with his approachable charisma. Margie leaned in closer, seizing the moment. "You know, it wouldn't hurt to see you and Luke together more often," she said, her voice dropping to a secretive whisper. "He's quite the handsome catch, isn't he?"

I sighed, a familiar frustration bubbling up. "Mom, can we not do this tonight?" I asked, my patience wearing thin. "I'm not interested in starting anything. Especially not with Luke. And especially not now. I've got enough on my plate."

Margie's expression softened, a mix of disappointment and understanding crossing her features. "Alright, Dear, I won't meddle. But you can't blame a mother for wishing her daughter all the happiness in the world, can you?"

I forced a small smile, acknowledging her well-meaning intentions, even if they were misguided. "I know, Mom. And I love you for it. But let's just focus on enjoying tonight, okay? There's enough drama around without adding dating into the mix."

She nodded, though a glint of impish sneakiness remained in her eye, suggesting our conversation was far from over. But for now, she gave in and refocused on the crowd and the promise of a night full of poetry and community.

Ruby, who had been low-key observing, gave me a sympathetic grin. "Don't worry, Piper. Your secret's safe with us."

I laughed, thankful for Ruby's sense of humor. "I'm going to need all the allies I can get if I'm to survive my mom's matchmaking schemes."

Just as our laughter began to subside, Zoe made her way through the crowd, her presence immediately brightening our little assembly. "What's all this? Did I miss the unveiling of Maplebrook's next top couple?" she teased, slipping effortlessly into the conversation with her usual flair.

"Oh, just my mom trying to orchestrate my love life. Again," I rolled my eyes for emphasis, unable to suppress a smile at Zoe's timely arrival.

Margie, always up for a laugh, wagged her finger playfully. "It's up to someone to keep tabs on the romantic possibilities around here. Heaven knows you two are too busy being detectives to notice the eligible bachelors under your noses."

Zoe winked at me. "As the official sidekick in these detective escapades, I hereby declare that our focus is solely on solving mysteries. Romance can wait until after we've cracked the case. Besides, who has time for love when there's intrigue afoot?"

Ruby's laughter filled the air as she playfully glanced between Zoe and me. "I must say, I do enjoy your adventures. They're far more entertaining than the usual Maplebrook gossip. Just invite me to the movie premiere when your story hits the big screen."

As the event started, Zoe and I slipped away, wading through the lively crowd to find a good view. The event had fully come alive, with the enchanting rhythm of poetry floating through the air, captivating the senses of all those gathered beneath the gently- glowing lights.

We scoped out a spot off to the side of the stage where we could watch everyone without being too obvious. We chose this position not just to enjoy the night's performances, but with a specific purpose in mind: to keep an eye out for Miranda Clarke. From our secluded spot, we could see the stage clearly, the poets taking turns to weave their magic, drawing applause and murmurs of appreciation from the crowd.

"I hope she shows up soon," Zoe whispered, her voice low to blend with the background noise. "I don't like the idea of cornering her, but we need answers."

I nodded, feeling the heaviness of what we had to do. "Let's just try to keep it as civil as possible. Remember, we're here to ask questions, not to accuse."

Luke's voice suddenly crackled through the wire, a reminder of our serious task. "Stay focused, ladies. You're there to gather information, not make a scene."

While we waited, my mom and Ruby settled into the crowd, their earlier jokes replaced by excitement for what the night had in store.

Lottie socialized with everyone, and we could hear her laughter from our spot.

With the poetry readings, chit-chat, and glasses clinking, Zoe and I stayed alert. It wasn't long before we spotted Miranda, unmistakable with her elegant stride, navigating the edge of the crowd with a cheese plate in one hand and a glass of wine in the other, like she was about to host her own little soirée behind the stage.

"If it isn't Maplebrook's very own Gatsby," Zoe said under her breath, barely nodding towards Miranda. "Shall we crash her party?"

I stifled a laugh. "Only if we promise to compliment her choice in cheese. Let's go."

"Remember, be subtle," Luke's voice reminded us through the wire. "Don't let her suspect anything."

We tiptoed after her, our steps as discreet as possible, which in Zoe's case meant only a slight jingle with every step thanks to her assortment of bracelets. "Stealth mode, Zoe," I whispered, my voice laced with caution.

"I'm as stealthy as they come," she whispered back. "Like a ninja. A very fashionable, slightly noisy ninja."

Miranda vanished behind the stage, and we quickly tried to keep up without anyone noticing. But when we turned the corner, she wasn't there. "Did she vanish into thin air? Is there a secret wine and cheese club back here we don't know about?" Zoe scanned the area.

I peeked behind crates and looked around corners, half-expecting Miranda to pop out and scold us for ruining the surprise. "Maybe she's a magician on the side. The Great Mirandini, disappearing with snacks."

Our search turned increasingly fruitless, the humor of our situation fading as confusion set in. Just as we were about to retrace our steps, thinking maybe we'd lost her in the crowd, a sharp cry sliced through the night's ambiance.

"Someone call 911! I think she's dead!"

The words hit me like a physical blow, freezing me in place. Zoe and I exchanged a horrified look before rushing towards the source of the cry. The atmosphere instantly changed from festive to terrifying.

As we arrived, the sight greeting us was one I'd hoped never to see. Miranda lay still on the ground, her wine glass shattered beside her, the cheese plate forgotten.

"Piper, Zoe, what's going on?" Luke's voice crackled urgently through the wire. "Report back immediately!"

Zoe grabbed my hand, her grip tight. "Piper, what do we do?"

I swallowed hard, my mind racing. "We help. And then we find out who did this." I took a deep breath and spoke into the wire, "Luke, it's Miranda. She's down behind the stage. We need help here now."

"Stay where you are. I'm on my way," Luke responded, his voice steady but urgent.

Tonight was supposed to be about confronting Miranda, not *this*.

As the crowd started to assemble, a combination of perplexity and apprehension filled the air. Luke forcefully made his way through, his countenance grave as he assumed authority over the scene. My eyes met Luke's across the chaos, a silent vow passing between us. This changed everything. Our search for answers just took a wild and unexpected turn, catching Zoe and I completely off-guard.

Chapter Eleven

♥

The morning after Miranda's death felt surreal, as if the vibrant spirit of Maplebrook had been muted overnight. News of the tragedy had spread like wildfire, casting a shadow over Poetry Under the Stars and leaving the fate of the rest of the festival hanging in the balance. As I unlocked the doors to Books and Brew's usually energetic space, I couldn't help but notice the somber mood filling the air. Instead of the usual sounds of laughter and chatter, there were only hushed conversations and anxious glances.

Sitting behind the counter, I couldn't help but flashback to last year's fiasco - you know, the one where I threw an event with more enthusiasm than common sense. Picture me, buzzing with excitement, thinking I was the next big thing in small-town entertainment. Spoiler alert: I wasn't. And don't even get me started on my partner in crime, "Jerky Jon" - a guy so slick, he could've sold ice to penguins. Fast forward to now, and I was still digging myself out of a financial hole deeper than my coffee mug. With the festival hanging by a thread thinner than my last nerve, solving this case wasn't just about justice anymore - it was about keeping my beloved bookstore afloat. Time to put on my detective hat (probably covered in glitter, knowing me) and crack this case faster than I could down a triple espresso with a side of sugary pastries.

The sudden and shrill ring of the phone pierced through the quiet, interrupting my deep thoughts. My hand instinctively moved towards the receiver, knowing exactly who would be on the other end before I even picked it up. "Books and Brew, Piper speaking."

"Piper, Darling, have you heard? The whole town's in an uproar. Such a tragedy, Miranda being found like that. And at the festival! Can you believe it?" Margie's voice tumbled out of the phone, a cascade of concern mixed with an insatiable need for conversation.

I sighed, leaning back in my chair as I braced myself for the monologue which was sure to follow. "Zoe and I were there when they found her."

"Oh, it's just awful, isn't it? And in such a public place! The festival was supposed to be the year's highlight. Now, who knows what will happen? I told Ruby, 'This is exactly what happens in those detective novels Piper sells,' not that I expected it to occur in Maplebrook."

My mother's talent for talking without listening was truly remarkable. I took a deep breath. "Mom," I interjected, seizing a rare moment of silence in her barrage of words. "It's been a tough time for everyone, especially with the festival. We're all trying to figure out what to do next."

"Of course, dear. But you know, life goes on. We can't let this one terrible event define us. Maplebrook is stronger than that. *You're* stronger than that. And think of the stories you'll have for your customers!"

Classic Margie, always finding a silver lining even in the stormiest of times. I couldn't help but grin, feeling a little of the tension melt away. "Thanks, Mom. I'll remember that. And I will keep you updated on any book-worthy developments."

"You do that, Dear. And remember, I'm always here if you need an ear. You know how I love our chats." The warmth in her voice reminded me that, despite her quirks, her heart was always in the right place.

Jazz was a small source of comfort as I cradled him in my arms, his purring providing solace amidst my chaotic thoughts. Miranda's guilt had seemed like a solid lead, a thread we could pull to unravel the mystery entangling Maplebrook. Being wrong about it felt like stumbling in the dark, unsure of where the next step would lead.

Lottie, in her ever-efficient whirlwind of activity, paused to notice my subdued mood. "Don't worry, we'll figure something out."

I managed a wry smile, shifting Jazz in my arms as he sought a more comfortable position. "Let's brainstorm some cheerful topics. Got any ideas on how we can boost sales?" I asked, staring at the non-jingling store door. "I was thinking maybe a mystery-themed book club night or a discount day for local authors."

Lottie's face brightened, her entrepreneurial spirit ignited. "How about a 'Blind Date with a Book' event? We can wrap books in plain paper with only teasers written on the outside. Adds a bit of mystery and fun to picking a new read."

I smiled, the brilliant idea appealing to my love of both books and surprises. "Let's do it. It could be the distraction we all need right now." I felt a little bit better with plans to revive Books and Brew. It was time to change things up and take a fresh approach to the investigation. I put Jazz down and watched him strut away like he owned the joint before grabbing my phone.

Dialing Zoe, I anxiously tapped my fingers on the counter as the phone rang. When she answered, I jumped straight to the point. "Hey, how about we grab lunch at The Prairie Plate? There's a bit more we have to dig into, and it gives us another opportunity to chat casually with Charlie. Could be a good chance to observe him when he's not on guard. Plus, I could really use your insight—and maybe a bit of your courage."

"Sounds like a plan," came Zoe's voice, which was immediately supportive, laced with a hint of intrigue "I'm always up for a bit of culinary detective work. See you there."

As Zoe and I settled into our booth at The Prairie Plate, the warmth of the bustling restaurant felt like a small refuge from the chill of uncertainty which had settled over Maplebrook. We ordered our usual—two plates of the daily special, which today was a savory herb chicken Charlie was particularly proud of. As we waited, the conversation naturally drifted to the previous evening's events.

"The more I think about it, the less Miranda's death makes sense," I said, toying with the napkin on my lap.

Zoe leaned back, her expression pensive. "Yeah, it's all sorts of twisted. And with her gone, it feels like we're missing a big piece of the puzzle. What do you think happened?"

I sighed, my thoughts a whirlwind. "Honestly, I don't know. But I have this nagging feeling that whatever happened to Miranda, it's connected to the secrets Professor Emerson was about to uncover. It's like we're on the edge of a cliff, and every step takes us closer to the truth—or over the edge."

Our food showed up just then and ruined our guessing game. We both took a moment to appreciate the dishes before us, the familiar routine offering a brief distraction.

"Listen, after lunch, I'm thinking of heading over to the police station," I said, breaking the silence. "Maybe I can get Ruby to share some inside information. She's always been good about letting things slip when it's important."

A subtle quirk of her eyebrow and a hint of a smile betrayed Zoe's amusement. "Piper, your ability to charm information out of people should be classified as a covert advantage."

I chuckled, glad Zoe could bring some levity to even the most serious conversations. "It's worth a try. Maybe we can figure out how Miranda fits into all this, or at least get a step closer to understanding what's going on."

Halfway through our meal, Charlie made his usual rounds through the restaurant. "How's everything here? The chicken to your liking?" He wore a friendly smile on his face as he approached our table.

"It's fantastic," I replied, savoring the last bite on my plate. "You've outdone yourself as usual."

Zoe chimed in, her appreciation evident. "You've got a real talent, for sure."

After a moment of pleasant exchanges about the day's special and upcoming menu items, I steered the conversation toward the reason we were really there. "Charlie, we were just talking about everything that's happened recently—Miranda's murder, the professor's research. It's been quite unsettling for Maplebrook."

Charlie's expression sobered at the mention. "Yes, just shocking news."

Leisurely taking another bite of my chicken, I glanced up at him with an air of casual curiosity, while Zoe played with the edge of her napkin, absorbed in the conversation. "You know, Ethan gave us a little nudge to check out the archives yesterday. Ended up finding something pretty interesting about a development project Miranda was championing," I started, aiming for a tone which suggested casual gossip rather than investigative probing. "Kind of circled back to Professor Emerson's fascination with Thornhill's Grove. All very intriguing, especially with the little debates you two had recently. Were you aware of what Miranda was up to?"

Charlie paused, a hint of surprise breaking through his usually composed demeanor. "Miranda's projects? I caught wind of something along those lines, but didn't get the details," he said with a relaxed shrug, matching my nonchalant approach. "Professor Emerson, he was passionate about his Grove theories. Made for some lively discussions, that's for sure."

Zoe smirked playfully. "Seems like Thornhill's Grove is the spot for all the town's mysteries."

Charlie laughed at that, the tension momentarily lifted. "Despite the disagreements, Professor Emerson's theories were compelling, to say the least. Always a good debate with him."

As Charlie excused himself to attend to other diners, Zoe and I exchanged a quick, meaningful look. The casual banter with Charlie had peeled back another layer of the mystery surrounding Thornhill's Grove, leaving us with more questions than answers.

I set down my fork and pushed my plate aside. "I think it's time I head over to the police station. Maybe Ruby can shed some light on things. She's usually good for a piece of insider info or two."

Zoe gave me a determined nod, the gears already turning in her head. "I'll weave through town like a mystery gossip ninja. You'd be amazed at what people spill over a cup of coffee and a well-timed 'Oh, really?'"

I knew full well Zoe's version of 'subtle' often came with a side of theatrical flair. "Just don't go renting a ninja costume, okay? We're trying to keep a low profile, not start a flash mob."

"Where's the fun in that?" Zoe countered with a wink. "Fine, I'll keep the ninja moves to a minimum. For now. How about we rendezvous later and exchange what we've learned? I'll bring snacks."

"That's a deal," I said, already dreading and looking forward to what she might uncover with her unique blend of charm and nosiness. "And, Zoe? Try not to start any rumors about a ninja invasion, alright?"

"No promises," Zoe said, standing up from the table with a grin. "Maplebrook could use a little excitement."

Once I made sure Lottie was ready for Books and Brew's hopefully-busy afternoon, I headed to the police station. The quiet which greeted me upon entry felt out of place, even for Maplebrook. It hit me that the strange silence was because most of the staff were caught up in a double-murder investigation, which had never happened before in our calm town.

Ruby, a familiar face in unfamiliar circumstances, manned the front desk. Glancing around to confirm we were alone and not wanting to draw any unnecessary attention, I leaned in and whispered a cautious hello. "Got a minute?" I murmured, keeping my voice low, half-hoping the walls didn't have ears.

Ruby's face lit up with surprise and relief. With a quick glance over her shoulder to ensure no one else was within earshot, she leaned in.

"What brings you here?" she asked, mirroring my conspiratorial tone. "Don't tell me you're looking to add amateur sleuthing to your resume," she teased, her eyes twinkling with a blend of humor and curiosity.

"I might already have, unofficially," I offered Ruby a half-smile, leaning in closer. "I'm on a bit of a fact-finding mission. Anything you might be able to share about the case? Off the record, of course."

Ruby's gaze shifted left and right, ensuring our conversation remained just between us. "I really shouldn't," she whispered, the weight of her duty pressing down on her words. "But you and Zoe are trying to do good. Just promise me you'll be careful, okay? We're not dealing with a simple case here."

I nodded earnestly, appreciating her trust. "You have my word."

She took a deep breath. "Miranda's death... it was poison. The same type that killed Professor Emerson. And it looks like it was in the wine she had at the poetry event. Luke's taking it pretty hard; he's out there right now, questioning the caterers, trying to see if anyone noticed anything out of the ordinary."

The revelation hit me like an icy wave. The same poison, a chilling echo of Emerson's fate, now entwined Miranda's. "The wine..." I murmured, piecing together the grim puzzle. "That means the killer was there, at the event. Among all of us."

Ruby nodded solemnly. "And that's why Luke's combing through every detail, every witness. Whoever did this was clever and danger-ous."

A heavy silence filled the space as her words hung in the air. I thanked Ruby, swore to be cautious, and left the station with a heavy heart. The thought that the killer had been so close, mingling with the townsfolk under the guise of celebration, sent shivers down my spine. As I headed back to Books and Brew, the afternoon sun seemed dim-mer, the cheerful bustle of Maplebrook now overlaid with a shadow of suspicion and fear.

It was clear now more than ever this wasn't just a case to be solved; it was a warning that danger lurked much closer to home than any of us had realized.

After closing up the bookstore, Zoe, Lottie, and I decided to check out Thornhill's Grove ourselves. Armed with flashlights and an un-healthy dose of determination, we headed into the woods like we were auditioning for a low-budget mystery film.

"Alright, ladies," I said, trying to sound more confident than I felt, "let's find some clues. And maybe a hidden snack stash, because all this sleuthing is making me hungry."

Zoe, our resident daredevil, took the lead with gusto. "I've got my trusty flashlight and a burning desire to not faceplant in the dark. What could possibly go wrong?"

Lottie, ever the voice of reason, chimed in, "Just watch your step. This place has more holes than my attempts at baking a soufflé."

We wandered deeper into the grove, past Eliza Maplebrook's grave - because nothing says 'girls' night out' like a stroll through a historic cemetery. Then, bam! We spotted disturbed earth, fresh as morning dew. "Look at this," I said, pointing like I'd discovered buried treasure. "Someone's been digging. Matches the dirt on Dean's coat. Coincidence? I think not!"

Zoe, channeling her inner detective, found footprints fresher than my last cup of coffee. And Lottie, not to be outdone, discovered some treacherous gravel. Just then, Zoe nearly took a tumble on said gravel. "Whoa! Almost wiped out there. Watch out, it's slipperier than a buttered floor!"

And because the universe loves a good plot twist, we stumbled upon a shovel and metal detector. "Well, well, well," I mused, feeling very Sherlock-esque, "looks like someone's been treasure hunting. But what are they looking for? Buried secrets? Long-lost heirlooms?"

As we stood there, surrounded by trees and mystery, I couldn't help but think: this was either the start of a really great adventure, or the opening scene of a questionable mystery novel. Either way, I was going to need more caffeine to see it through.

Chapter Twelve

♥

Despite a restless night of analyzing every conversation and dead end, the morning sun at Books and Brew's windows provided a glimpse of normalcy amid chaos. Jazz never left my side as I got ready, his purring soothing my worries.

My gaze shifted toward him, his tail creating a soft, sweeping motion through the air. "What do you think, Jazz? Got any clues for us?" I half-joked, allowing a small smile despite the gravity of recent events. I longed for Jazz to offer any clue at all which could help uncover the mysterious darkness shrouding Maplebrook.

Right then, the bookstore's door swung open and in walked Zoe, bringing a burst of fresh air and a boost of energy. Her vibrant spirit was undiminished, but her eyes quickly sought mine, reflecting a shared concern. "How's our leading lady in this real-life mystery drama?" With a mix of cheerfulness and seriousness, she playfully greeted Jazz.

I couldn't help but smile back, despite the weight of my concerns. "Worried," I confessed, straightening up and facing her. "If the festival ends early because of the murders, Books and Brew might not make it through the season. We need to figure this out, and soon."

Zoe's smile faded, replaced by a look of determination. "I've been thinking," she said, her voice taking on a serious tone. "We should talk to Dean again. He was close to both Miranda and the professor. Maybe we missed something the first time around."

I nodded. Dean, the curator of the Historical Museum, was indeed a link to both victims. It was time for a second visit.

After making sure Lottie was good at the cafe, Zoe and I found ourselves back at the Historical Museum, ready to dig deeper into Dean's connections with Miranda and Professor Emerson.

Dean greeted us with a cautious warmth. "You ladies back again? To what do I owe the pleasure?" His tone seemed polite but guarded.

"We did some digging into that development project Miranda was pushing for," I started, trying to sound as nonchalant as possible while Zoe stood supportively next to me. "Came across her involvement with Thornhill's Grove. You and the professor had some lively debates over that, didn't you? Did you know about Miranda's plans?"

Dean hesitated, then sighed. "Miranda was ambitious, had her sights set on a few projects, but I can't say I was privy to the details. As for Emerson, yes, we had our differences, but it was all professional."

Zoe, ever ready to lighten the mood, chimed in. "Seems like Thornhill's Grove is the place to be for Maplebrook's history buffs."

Dean chuckled at the suggestion, the tension momentarily easing. "Perhaps. Though, Professor Emerson was certainly onto something with his research. It's a pity we'll never truly know what he discovered."

Dean's laughter, while light, didn't fully mask the undercurrent of unease which lingered in the air. Zoe, sensing a chance, leaned in, super curious. "You mentioned his research. It must have stirred quite the pot. Any memorable reactions from the town folks?"

Dean hesitated, his gaze drifting momentarily to a spot behind us as if lost in thought. "Yes, the Professor's findings were controversial at times. Not everyone appreciated his perspective on Maplebrook's history..." he admitted, his voice trailing off slightly.

I nudged the conversation gently, hoping to unearth more. "Controversial how?"

"It's not my place to spread rumors," Dean started, his tone cautious. Yet, after a brief pause, something seemed to shift within him, a decision made. "But since you're asking and given the circumstances..." He cleared his throat. "There was an incident. A rather heated argument between Miranda and an unidentified man, right here in the museum. This was a few days before--before her unfortunate passing."

Zoe and I exchanged a glance, the significance of Dean's revelation not lost on us. "An unidentified man? Did you hear anything specific? About Emerson's research, maybe?"

Dean seemed uncomfortable, rubbing the back of his neck. "I didn't catch the entire conversation, but it was tense. Miranda was quite upset, and the man, he was insistent. He mentioned Thornhill's Grove, and she said something about 'correcting the record.' It was clear he had strong, opposing views."

I furrowed my brow, pressing for more details. "What did this man look like? Anything you can remember might help."

Dean shook his head slowly. "It was hard to see him clearly. He kept to the shadows, like he didn't want to be recognized. He was wearing a dark coat, and a hat pulled over his face. I remember thinking he looked out of place, because it was too nice of a day to have on such a heavy coat."

"What about hair color? Or facial features?" Zoe chimed in, her curiosity piqued.

Dean frowned, trying to recall. "He had dark hair, I think, but it was hard to tell with the hat. His face was mostly in shadow."

I took a deep breath, processing the information. "Did you hear anything specific about their argument? Any clues about what they were fighting over?"

Dean shook his head again. "Not really, just bits and pieces. The man mentioned Thornhill's Grove several times, and Miranda kept insisting on 'correcting the record,' whatever that means. It sounded like it was about more than just the history of the town."

"Do you think he was connected to Emerson's research?" Zoe asked, her voice tense with urgency.

"It's possible," Dean admitted. "But I couldn't say for sure. All I know is that Miranda seemed genuinely frightened, and that's not something I've ever seen in her before."

"Thank you, Dean," I said, giving him a reassuring smile. "You've been a big help. We'll get to the bottom of this."

Dean nodded, still looking uneasy. "Just be careful, alright? There's a lot more at stake here than meets the eye."

As we left the museum, Zoe and I felt a new energy in the air. The discovery of an argument, a mysterious man, added another layer to the complexity of the case. Maplebrook's peaceful exterior was slowly unraveling, exposing its hidden secrets through each whispered conversation.

"Looks like we've got more digging to do," Zoe remarked, her voice a mix of excitement and resolve.

"Let's hope this leads us closer to the truth," I replied.

Zoe went back to Palette Whispers to catch up on work and get more town gossip, while I headed to Books and Brew, deep in thought about our chat with Dean. The mention of a heated argument between Miranda and an unidentified man had added a new layer of complexity to the puzzle.

As I was turning onto Cedar Lane, I almost ran into Luke. Coming in the opposite direction, he had a furrowed brow and his eyes were fixed on the ground, as if he was hoping to find a solution to the case from the very pavement beneath his feet. He glanced up and narrowed his eyes, stopping me in my tracks. His face showed how frustrated he was, which was completely opposite to the peacefulness of our little town. It was clear the murders had caused a lot of turmoil.

"Piper," Luke began, his voice a mixture of frustration and concern. "I was just on my way to Books and Brew. I wanted to talk to you and get your take on what happened last night."

I took a deep breath, getting ready for the conversation we had to have, even though I really didn't want to. "I was going to come see you after checking in at Books and Brew."

He ran his hand through his hair, which I knew meant he was stressed. "This investigation, it's like every turn we take, we hit another dead end. It's frustrating, and seeing you and Zoe out there, trying to do my job—"

"It's not like that, Luke," I interrupted, hoping to cut through his building irritation. "We're just trying to help. This town, my store... they mean everything to me. And after last night, I'm even more worried about what this all means for its future."

For a moment, Luke's stern facade softened, and he looked at me not just as a detective to a civilian but as one person concerned for another. "I get that, Piper. I do. It's just been...overwhelming," Luke finished, his gaze meeting mine with a level of sincerity I hadn't seen in him before. "This case, it's big, and there is a lot of pressure on me. And since I'm new around here, people don't really want to open up to me."

I nodded, realizing the pressure he was dealing with. The urge to share what Zoe and I had just learned from Dean pressed against my lips, a potential lead which could help Luke in his investigation. "Actually, that's part of why I wanted to talk to you. We learned something from Dean at the museum," I said, gauging his reaction. He seemed open. "He mentioned witnessing a heated argument between Miranda and some unknown man just a few days before...you know."

Luke's frustration shifted into sharp focus, his detective instincts kicking in. "An unknown man?" he echoed, his tone sharpening with interest. "Dean saw this? Why didn't he come forward sooner?"

"I'm not sure," I admitted. "But it got me thinking—maybe there's someone else we should be looking into. Someone who had motives we haven't considered yet."

After a moment of consideration, Luke's face took on a contemplative look. "That's... actually helpful, Piper. Thank you. I'll need to follow up with Dean on this. See if we can identify this man."

The tension between us eased slightly, replaced by a mutual understanding of the challenges we faced. "I just want to help, Luke," I said, my voice softening. "Maplebrook means as much to me as it does to you. We all want the same thing—to find out who's responsible for this."

Luke acknowledged with a nod, as the lines of frustration faded from his face. "I know you do. And I appreciate it, Piper. Let's keep this line of communication open, alright? If you or Zoe come across anything else, no matter how insignificant it might seem, let me know. But be careful. If the murderer is still in town and he/she gets wind you're looking into things, you may be next."

As I returned to Books and Brew, I couldn't help but perceive Luke in a different manner. His genuine concern and unexpected openness left me with a blend of optimism and unease regarding the future.

The quaint streets of Maplebrook, usually a source of comfort, now whispered secrets and hidden dangers with every step.

Upon returning, Lottie greeted me with her usual vibrant energy, though it dimmed slightly as she shared the business had been slower than usual. "People seem a bit wary of community events these days," she sighed, fussing over the display by the window.

Jazz, sensing the shift in mood, leaped onto the counter, offering his silent support with a soft purr.

I stroked his fur, mulling over Lottie's words. "It's understandable, I guess. But we'll get through this. We always do."

Lottie perked up, her enthusiasm undiminished by the challenges. "Before I forget, Sophie swung by earlier, fishing for a 'comment' for her next article. But don't worry, I gave her the Lottie special—told her our focus is on community spirit, not sensationalism."

I laughed, picturing the scene. "What would we do without you?"

"Speaking of community spirit," Lottie's mood perked up even more as she motioned towards a bunch of books on the counter, each one wrapped in plain brown paper with a twine bow. "I've been working on the 'Blind Date with a Book' event. Thought it might bring a bit of mystery and joy back. People could use it, don't you think?"

I admired the neatly-wrapped books, each promising an unknown adventure. The sight of them, each adorned with a simple twine bow, sparked something inside me—a mixture of admiration for Lottie's ever-creative mind and a flicker of hope the "Blind Date with a Book" event could indeed be the catalyst to bring a little light back to Maplebrook and, selfishly, a much-needed boost to Books and Brew's sales.

I picked up one of the packages, feeling its weight and wondering about the story hidden within. "In times like these, a bit of mystery and the joy of discovery might be just what people need to feel connected again, to feel a part of the community despite...well, everything."

Lottie beamed, clearly pleased. "Exactly my thoughts! And who knows, it might even get more people through the door, eager for a surprise read and a cup of coffee."

I returned the book to the counter, my mind already buzzing with ideas to promote the event and attract both our regulars and newbies. "Let's make sure everyone knows about it. We could use the bulletin board, social media, and maybe even get Sophie to write something positive for a change."

Jazz, ever the inquisitive one, hopped onto the counter to inspect the mysterious packages, his nose twitching as he sniffed at the bows. "Seems like Jazz is ready to sign up for his own blind date," I joked, earning a soft meow in response, as if he agreed.

Lottie's infectious laughter and optimism lingered in the air long after she had made her promise to spread the word about our new "Blind Date with a Book" event. Her enthusiasm was like a ray of sunshine, just like the smell of fresh coffee at Books and Brew. "Trust me, Piper, it's going to be great," she reassured me with a smile before heading out, leaving the café quieter in her absence.

As the sun went down and cast long shadows, the last customers left, thanking us and saying goodbye. The café settled into a peaceful lull, a stark contrast to the hustle and bustle of the day. Jazz, the protector of Books and Brew, staked out his ideal spot on the windowsill. He casually watched people stroll by, his tail playfully twitching in the sun.

As I tidied up Books and Brew, the thought of "Blind Date with a Book" gave me hope. With every swipe of the tables and each chair adjustment, I silently prayed the event would revive interest and bring the community together.

The warmth of the setting sun through the café windows did little to ease the chill of worry which had settled deep in my bones. Even with Lottie's contagious positivity and Jazz's comforting company, I worried about the festival's fate and how everyone in Maplebrook looked worried. It could tear apart everything I tried to create in Books and Brew.

It was amidst these reflections, my mind a whirlwind of figures and forecasts, that my phone's sudden buzz jolted me back to reality. I frowned, pulling the device from my pocket, expecting perhaps a message from Zoe about any new gossip she'd gathered. Instead, what I found sent a chill down my spine. An anonymous message, stark against the glowing screen: *Be careful, Piper. You're treading on dangerous ground. Not all secrets are meant to be uncovered.*

I stared at the note, reading it over and over, trying to make sense of it. Who could have sent it? And how much did they know about our investigation? The warning was vague, yet its implications were clear—someone was watching us, someone who wanted to keep the truth hidden.

Chapter Thirteen

♥

Lottie and I were up before the sun, getting Books and Brew ready for the day. It was still cold, but we warmed up the place with lights and the delicious smell of brewing coffee. Jazz, as if sensing the start of a new day, darted through the café with a case of the zoomies, his black and white fur a blur against the warm backdrop of bookshelves and cozy chairs.

I grabbed the coffee pot and poured myself a cup of liquid strength. The strong brew was my daily shield against all the uncertainties. Lottie, happily humming a tune despite the gloomy mood in Maplebrook, grabbed one of Evie's famous blueberry scones—a tasty little comfort in the chaos.

"Imagine the life of a cat," I said, as Jazz finally stopped, catching his breath. "Oblivious to murder mysteries and only concerned with his next sprint."

Lottie laughed, her voice shining in the morning's half-light. Wish we could trade places for a day. I'd be an amazing cat, you know. I'm really good at taking naps and judging the world."

Her lighthearted comment made me smile, at least for a moment. "But then who would make our coffee? Jazz certainly hasn't mastered the art of brewing."

As our laughter subsided, the reality of our situation crept back in. I hesitated and pulled out my phone, showing Lottie the anonymous message I had received the night before. "Someone's playing games, and I can't tell if it's a warning...or a threat."

Lottie's expression got serious when she read the message, her playful mood turning to worry. "This is serious, Piper. Whoever sent it knows what we're up to. Maybe it's time to take a step back?"

I sighed, staring into the depths of my coffee cup as if it held the answers. "I wish I could, but stepping back feels like letting them win. We need to be smart about this, smarter than we've been so far."

Jazz, all recovered and full of energy, hopped onto the counter, looking at us with his green eyes like he was trying to understand how serious things were. "Looks like we're going to need all the help we can get," I said, scratching his head gently. "Even if it's just moral support from a cat with the zoomies."

As the morning went on, Books and Brew got thankfully busy with customers looking for their usual coffee and contemplation. Lottie and I moved seamlessly through the space, the rhythm of opening day now second nature to us. Jazz, happy with his previous adventures, plopped down in his favorite sunbeam, chilling on the counter and watching the world.

The soft sound of the doorbell jingling filled the air as Sophie Turner stepped inside. Her determined walk and purposeful gaze were as familiar to me as the scent of freshly-brewed coffee in the morning. Holding a notebook, she made her way to the counter, her reporter's gaze locked onto me.

"Morning, Sophie. Can I get you a coffee? Lemon poppyseed muffin?" I asked, hoping to distract her from whatever inane questions she came to hassle me with. "Fresh just this morning from Evie's."

She shook her head and waved me off. "Watching the figure." She glanced at my carefully chosen outfit – a graphic tee with a whimsical cat reading a book – just the right amount of color and somberness to match the double-murder aftermath. "It's wonderful how you always manage to find something that fits, having all these lovely treats around."

I managed a polite smile, though her comment stung more than I cared to admit. "Moderation is everything, isn't it? But thank you, I appreciate the thought." I poured myself a cup of coffee and fantasized about spilling it on her crisp, ivory suit. "What brings you in today?"

She flipped open her little notepad and tapped her pen on the paper. "With all that's been happening, how has business been? Any comments on the impact of the recent events on Books and Brew?" Her tone walked the line between professional curiosity and personal concern.

I shrugged, maintaining a nonchalant facade. There was no way I was going to let Sophie know how much the recent events had affected Books and Brew, and she was likely to just rub it in. For some reason, we'd never really gotten along, and I wasn't about to give her something to gloat over.

"We're holding up, just like the town. Maplebrook's strong; we don't let a little mystery scare us off our coffee," I said, trying to keep the atmosphere light.

"If anything, we've had more people stopping by," said Lottie, piping up from where she was arranging a display of new books. "Nothing like a bit of intrigue to spark interest in a good mystery novel, right?"

It was Sophie's turn to chuckle, though her eyes remained sharp, always searching for the deeper story. "You won't believe the anonymous tip I got this morning about Charlie's family," she said, leaning in closer. "Seems like there's something else going on besides just an academic disagreement with Professor Emerson."

The casual mention of the tip caught me off guard, my attempt at nonchalance faltering. Lottie looked over, intrigued. "An anonymous tip seems awfully convenient. What's the scoop?"

Sophie hesitated, as if weighing the wisdom of sharing. "It seems like Charlie's family could be tangled up in a land dispute that Emerson's research might blow open. Evidently, there is more on the line than simply maintaining historical accuracy."

I exchanged a quick look with Lottie, both of us processing the implications. "Interesting," I mused aloud. "But why come to you with this, Sophie? And why now?"

The journalist shrugged, a gesture suggesting both frustration and determination. "Who knows why people share what they do? But it's my job to follow up. If there's truth to it, it could shed new light on the case."

Sophie's departure from Books and Brew was as purposeful as her entrance - a smooth, confident stride carrying her towards the door. As the door swung shut, the silence following seemed charged with the weight of her news. Lottie, who had observed from the sidelines, pushed away from the counter where she had been leaning and let out a long, exasperated sigh.

"With all these pieces floating around, don't you think we need to get a bit more organized with our investigation?"

The word 'investigation' from Lottie made everything feel serious, even though we hadn't said it out loud before. I paused, considering her suggestion. The idea resonated with me, echoing thoughts I hadn't fully admitted to myself. "You might be onto something. We're really detectives at this point, aren't we?"

Lottie nodded, her expression earnest. "What if we made it official? Like a secret club or something?"

A smile tugged at my lips, the absurdity and brilliance of the idea striking me simultaneously. "A club, huh? How about 'The Murder Mystery Book Club'?" The name felt right, capturing the essence of our literary-themed sleuthing.

Lottie's eyes lit up, and even Jazz seemed to approve, meowing his assent from his spot by the window. "I love it. It sounds just mysterious enough to be intriguing," Lottie agreed, her earlier concerns momentarily dispelled by the excitement of our new venture.

"That settles it," I said, feeling a surge of determination. I pulled out my phone, quickly composing a message to Zoe. "I'm texting Zoe. We'll need all hands on deck if we're going to get to the bottom of this."

Books and Brew felt different after Sophie left, with an intangible tension which lingered in the air. The door had chimed softly upon her departure, sealing us back in our own little coffee and book bubble, now filled with hushed conspiracies. I took a deep breath, the reality of our situation sinking in. We were in deep—deeper than I'd ever imagined when I first set out to help solve our town's murders.

The café was quiet now, the usual bustle of the day settling into the calm of evening. As the sun set, the shadows grew longer and the warm lights made the space even cozier, perfect for sneaky meetings.

Zoe arrived not long after Lottie and I closed for the day. "So, what's the big emergency?" she asked, half-joking as she slid into a chair opposite me at the back table we'd commandeered for our "official meeting." It was away from prying eyes and possible nosey customers, although none had graced my doorstep for over an hour.

I shared Sophie's tip about Charlie's family and the land dispute, watching Zoe's expression change from curiosity to worry. "What's our play?" she asked, ready to dive into action.

Pulling a whiteboard closer, I uncapped a marker. "Let's review everything we've got," I said, as we tried to piece together the puzzle of clues, suspects, and theories. The names Dean, Ethan, and now Charlie, along with Sophie's anonymous tip, took center stage on our board.

"We need more info on this land thing," Zoe said, looking puzzled. "But we go in quietly. Old newspapers, the archives, maybe a chat or two with some of the town's older residents."

I nodded in agreement. "And we avoid direct confrontation with Charlie for now. The last thing we need is to tip our hand too soon."

Just when we thought it couldn't get any crazier, Jazz, the silent observer, jumped on the table and almost knocked over a stack of notes. Zoe chuckled, gently placing him back on the ground. "Looks like we've got our work cut out for us, team."

As we talked more about our plan, I felt both the weight of responsibility and a spark of excitement. The Murder Mystery Book Club was officially in session.

The next day seemed like a treasure hunt through Maplebrook's past, chasing after ghosts instead of real clues. Jazz shot me a look when he realized I was leaving early. It was a mix of curiosity and caution. I gave him a reassuring pat and promised to come back with answers, hoping today would clear things up.

"Sorry, buddy," I said, stroking him lightly under the chin. "Extra treats when I get back, promise."

The library was so quiet, which made the chaos in my head stand out even more. Nora, the librarian who had become a familiar face over the years, greeted me with a smile which was both welcoming and knowing.

"Back for more mystery solving, Piper?" she asked, her glasses sliding down the bridge of her nose as she peered over them.

"Not so loud, Nora," I said, looking around as I dropped my list of questions on the counter. "I was hoping to get access to the archives. We're looking into a land dispute involving the Alderton family and something called Thornhill's Grove. Ring any bells?"

Nora paused, her expression thoughtful. "The Aldertons, yes...a family with deep roots and long shadows in Maplebrook. But Thornhill's Grove? That's a bit more obscure. Let's see what we can find."

She took me to the archives, a room which smelled like old paper and hidden secrets. We wasted hours going through dusty boxes and microfiche with no real results.

"I'm sorry," Nora finally said, her disappointment mirroring my own. "There's mention of the Aldertons, of course, and countless land disputes over the years, but nothing specific to Thornhill's Grove. It's as if it's been deliberately erased from the records."

I leaned back, rubbing my tired eyes. "I just know I'm missing something."

Nora smiled sympathetically. "History has a way of hiding its secrets, Piper. Sometimes, it's the smallest detail that cracks the case wide open."

With a heavy heart, I thanked Nora for her help and left the library. Today only left me with more questions, making me doubt if I'd ever find the answers. Heading back to Books and Brew, the investigation seemed even heavier. Today was tough, but I wasn't about to give up. All I could do for now was find Zoe and Lottie and hope one of them had the breakthrough we desperately needed.

"It's like looking for a needle in a mountain of books," Zoe lamented, staring at the sparse information we'd gathered. Her frustration evident, she sank into one of the cozy chairs scattered around Books and Brew, her vibrant energy dimmed.

I nodded, feeling the weight of our fruitless efforts. Jazz, sensing our dejection, hopped onto Zoe's lap, offering his own form of comfort as he curled up, purring softly. "At least someone's having a good day," Zoe remarked, a small smile breaking through as she stroked his fur.

Lottie joined us, setting down a tray with freshly-brewed coffee and a plate of Evie's blueberry scones. "I've been all ears today, but it seems like everyone's tight-lipped. Or maybe they're just as in the dark as we are."

"We did our best," I said, trying to muster optimism. "Zoe, anything from the art shop?"

With a rueful expression, Zoe shook her head. "There's some gossip going around about the Aldertons and some land problems, but nothing definite. Just a bunch of speculation. How about you, Lottie? Any luck here?"

Lottie sighed, accepting a cup of coffee. "There's plenty of interest in the murders, but no one seems to know much about Thornhill's Grove. It's like we're chasing shadows."

"I guess it's back to the drawing board," I finally said, breaking the silence. "We might need to rethink our approach. Maybe there's another angle we haven't considered yet to avoid more dead ends."

Zoe's eyes sparkled with a mix of mischief and resolve. "Dead ends? More like just the scenic route to the truth. And let's face it, with the 'Murder Mystery Book Club' on the case, it's only a matter of time before we crack it wide open. And we've got Jazz, the coolest cat detective in town."

Lottie chuckled, her optimism as infectious as ever. "I've heard cats are excellent at uncovering secrets. Right, Jazz? Think you can sniff out our mystery culprit for us?" Jazz merely blinked slowly, his purring uninterrupted, as if to say, "If only you knew."

Their energy lifted my spirits. Even with all the ups and downs, there was a fun excitement in the chase, a sense of camaraderie from our amateur sleuthing. "Well, team, it looks like we've got more work to do. Let's show this town what the 'Murder Book Club' is made of."

Zoe raised her coffee cup in a mock salute. "To uncovering secrets and the best darn book club Maplebrook's ever seen."

"And to Jazz, our secret weapon," Lottie added. "May his whiskers guide us to victory."

Just as we were about to call it a night, my phone buzzed with an anonymous message that again chilled me to the bone: *Be careful, Piper. You're playing a dangerous game.*

Chapter Fourteen

♥

After the chilling message left no doubt that our little "Murder Mystery Book Club" had rattled some cages, Zoe, Lottie, and I convened at Books and Brew for an emergency session the next morning. The morning light seeped through the windows, creating a hopeful ambiance as we sat around the table with our coffee cups, pastries, and a chaotic mix of notes and documents. Jazz was snuggled up in a chair nearby, his purring providing a soothing soundtrack to our hectic preparations.

"I can't believe someone's actually threatening us," Zoe whispered, sounding a bit scared as she read the creepy message on my phone again.

"It means we're onto something," I said, trying to fake some confidence. "That's even more reason to keep going."

Lottie nodded, her expression stern yet supportive. "We just need to be smart and cautious. Let's go over everything again, see if we've missed something."

With that, we acted as if we were closing for the night and shut the bookstore's blinds. I was careful to go upstairs in my apartment and turn on some lights, acting as if I were getting ready for bed. Back downstairs, we dove into the evidence, approaching our investigation with fresh eyes. I came up with a new plan. "How about we make a timeline? Lay out everything we know, piece by piece. It could help us spot connections we missed."

Everyone was on board with the idea, so we started making laying everything out. As the timeline got longer, a faint but definite pattern began to emerge.

While we were huddled around the table in Books and Brew, piecing together our clues, I decided to do a bit of online digging. I pulled out my laptop and began searching through the city's digital archives, hoping to find something we had missed.

As I carefully reconstructed everything, I discovered an old town hall meeting transcript from the city's website where Charlie Alderton passionately opposed a development project near Thornhill's Grove. His words, once dismissed as mere local politics, now shimmered with potential significance.

In the transcript, Charlie Alderton objected passionately, expressing his deep concerns about the proposed development near Thornhill's Grove. He argued that the project would ruin the environment and destroy important history in Maplebrook.

Charlie's statement read: *This development project represents more than just a change in our landscape; it's a direct assault on the very fabric of our town's history. Thornhill's Grove isn't just another plot of land—it's a key to our past, holding stories and truths that we've yet to uncover. By paving over it, we're not just losing green space; we're losing chapters of our collective story, ones that could redefine how we see ourselves and our founding families.*

His plea to reconsider the development in light of potential historical significance highlighted his respect for Emerson's research, despite their known disagreements. *"I've had my differences with Professor Emerson,"* Charlie continued. *"But on this, he and I see eye to eye. There's something there, beneath the Grove, that belongs to all of us, a heritage we're on the verge of discovering. We owe it to ourselves and future generations to protect that chance."*

Charlie's passion and plea to save rather than build resonated with a few council members, but it didn't stop the project completely. But he really believed the Grove was important and finding history was more important than anything else. This made his objections really important to look at again after the murders happened.

Zoe broke the silence first, her voice tinged with uncertainty. "If Charlie was this passionate about preserving Thornhill's Grove, aligning with Emerson's research, it doesn't quite add up, does it? Him being our killer, I mean."

I nodded, my thoughts mirroring hers. "His stance at the town hall meeting was about safeguarding the grove, not destroying it. Professor Emerson's findings could have bolstered Charlie's arguments against the development. Killing him would have been counterproductive. But what exactly was Thornhill Grove's history? Why was it so important to Emerson and Charlie?"

Lottie, ever practical, chimed in, stirring her tea thoughtfully. "So Charlie and Professor Emerson might have actually been on the same page, at least regarding the grove. That doesn't sound like a motive for murder to me."

"The plot thickens when you add Miranda into the mix," I continued, piecing together the narrative. "She was pushing for the development project, right in the heart of what Charlie and, presumably, Professor Emerson were trying to protect. It puts her at odds with both of them."

Zoe leaned forward, her detective instincts kicking in. "So Charlie's outburst was probably more out of desperation than anger. Miranda's project jeopardized everything he was fighting for."

"And if Miranda was eliminated," Lottie added, her voice dropping to a whisper. "It might have been to silence her, to stop the project, not because she knew too much about Professor Emerson's death."

The realization settled over us like a fog. Things got complicated when the dynamics we thought were happening turned out to be a tangled mess of motives and opportunities.

I sighed, feeling the weight of our discoveries. "We need to tread carefully. If Charlie isn't our guy, and Miranda's death was about stopping the development rather than her knowledge of Professor Emerson's murder, we're looking at a very different kind of killer."

Zoe nodded solemnly. "Someone who's playing a long game, manipulating events from the shadows. We're not just solving a murder; we're uncovering a conspiracy that's rooted deep in Maplebrook's soil."

Chapter Fifteen

♥

With coffee in one hand and a marker in the other, I found myself in front of the whiteboard at Books and Brew just as the sun was rising. The others had left, but our timeline felt like it was dragging on forever, with each suspect and piece of evidence just adding to the confusion, and I couldn't let it go. Jazz was the only one keeping me company, purring softly by my feet, a constant comfort in the midst of my racing thoughts.

"We completely overlooked the footprint," I whispered, more to myself than to Jazz, who sat attentively at my feet, his tail wrapping around him like a question mark.

The realization hit me hard. In all the chaos of clues and suspects, we'd forgotten about the footprint we found near the scene. Jazz looked up, his green eyes wide and curious, but he wasn't exactly springing into action. Instead, he flopped down at my feet, rolling over to present his belly in a move which clearly said, 'Forget about footprints, what about belly rubs?'

I chuckled, giving into his silent demand and rubbing his tummy as he rolled from one side to the other. "You know, Jazz, if you were half as interested in solving crimes as you are in belly rubs, we'd have this case wrapped up by now."

His only response was to purr even louder, not caring in the slightest about the recent events in Maplebrook or the financial impact on Books and Brew. Hmpf, maybe if his treat supply dwindled he would care a little more, I thought to myself.

With a shake of my head, I rose to my feet, my focus shifting back to the investigation. "But seriously, Jazz, what did Luke find out about the footprint? It could be a game-changer."

Jazz offered no insights, content in his world of stretches and scratches. With a resigned sigh, I realized I wouldn't get the answers I needed from my furry companion. "Looks like it's up to me, then," I grabbed my bag. "Time for a little trip to the police station. Maybe Ruby can shed some light on this." And with one last pat for Jazz, I headed out, determined to chase down the lead we'd all but forgotten.

On my way, I veered towards the bakery, lured in by the comforting aroma of freshly-baked goods filling the air. "Hey, Evie," I called out as I entered, greeted by the sight of rows upon rows of tempting pastries.

"Good morning, Piper. What can I get for you today?" she asked, ready to box up my order.

"I'll take a dozen mixed donuts, a bit of everything," I said, my gaze lingering on the display case. "And a slice of your banana bread for me. Can't start the day without a proper breakfast, right?"

Evie expertly arranged a variety of donuts into a box. "No doubt about it. This will keep you fueled."

The mix had it all - classic glazed, rich chocolate frosted, and those jam-filled treasures which always vanished first. With a beaming smile, she gleefully handed me the warm scone, its sweet aroma instantly filling me with delight and happiness.

"Thanks, Evie. This is exactly what I needed," I said, grabbing the box and my bread, ready to rock the day. The early morning was the best time to swing by the police station, and I hoped Evie's tasty donuts would convince Ruby to chat.

The police department was quiet as I walked in, the early hour ensuring only a skeleton crew was present. "Morning, Ruby," I greeted, sliding the box across her desk with a hopeful smile. "Brought you guys some breakfast. Any chance you've got a minute?"

Ruby's eyes sparkled when she saw the donuts and she hurriedly took me to a private room, away from anyone who might be listening. My visit was a long shot, but with the festival on standstill and Books and Brew's future at stake, I was willing to try anything to find the truth.

I lowered my voice to a conspiratorial whisper. "That footprint we found near where Professor Emerson...well, you know. Any chance the lab results came back yet?"

Making sure we weren't overheard, Ruby glanced around before leaning in closer. "Actually, yes." Her eyes alight with the thrill of sharing confidential information. "They did a soil analysis. There were some unique traces of dirt, not really common around here. It's apparently specific to the area around Thornhill's Grove—"

My heart skipped a beat. "Thornhill's Grove? That's where Professor Emerson's research was all about!"

Ruby nodded, her expression serious. "It doesn't prove who did it, but it definitely narrows down where they've been. There just aren't that many folks who have reason to wander around there."

"Thornhill's Grove isn't exactly a hotspot," I said, mulling over Ruby's words. "Most people stay away unless they have a specific reason to be there, like paying respects at Eliza Maplebrook's grave or for historical tours. It's not exactly the town's favorite picnic spot."

Ruby nodded, her expression serious. "Exactly. So if someone's been spending time there recently, especially around the area where

Professor Emerson was focusing his research, it could be a significant lead."

"Then we need to find out who's been there and why," I said, feeling a surge of determination.

Ruby looked worried. "Just be careful."

With this new information in hand, my mind raced with the possibilities. The soil composition directly connected the footprint to Thornhill's Grove, indicating the person who left it had been to the same place Professor Emerson and maybe Miranda were exploring. This wasn't just a clue; it was a guiding light pointing us in the direction to understand how the killer moved and what drove him.

"Thanks, Ruby. This—this could be big," I managed, my thoughts already turning to how this evidence could reshape our investigation.

As I left the station, Ruby's bombshell kept replaying in my head, linking the murders to Thornhill's Grove in a whole new way.

As I made my way back to Books and Brew, my mind raced with possibilities. The Grove, the footprint, the development project—how did they fit into the puzzle of the murders? And more importantly, how could we, a makeshift team of curious entrepreneurs trying to survive, make sense of it all without crossing lines we couldn't uncross?

I walked into the café and there was Lottie, arranging the books like a pro. Jazz greeted me with a stretch and a yawn, looking like he was ready for a nap. Watching him, I couldn't help but envy his ability to find peace amidst the chaos swirling around us.

"How did it go at the police station?" Lottie asked, pausing momentarily.

I poured myself a big cup of coffee and drowned it in cream and sugar. After devouring the banana bread earlier, I should've been done with sugar. But no, the situation called for a sweetness overload—a necessary fuel for the brewing storm in my brain.

I took a sip of my now borderline-diabetic concoction. "Let's just say the plot thickens, and not in a good way." I recounted the gist of Ruby's information, alluding to the footprint and its ties to Thornhill's Grove. Lottie absorbed every word, her brow furrowing with concern.

Jazz apparently thought it was the perfect time to claim a spot on the counter, settling down near the cash register with a soft thud. I guess he thought he was the boss of our brainstorming session.

"But hey," I continued, flashing a grin I hoped conveyed more confidence than I felt. "On the bright side, this whole murder mystery gig is giving me ideas for a new 'Books and Brew After Dark' series. Nothing like a good, old-fashioned whodunit to keep the cash register ringing, right?"

Lottie grinned, shaking her head. "Only you, Piper. Only you could find a silver lining in all of this. But you're right, we can't give up. Books and Brew needs us."

Chapter Sixteen

♥

"D id you see this?" Zoe's voice broke the silence in the café as she slammed a copy of the Maplebrook Herald on the counter. Her finger jabbed at the headline: *"Secret Society's Shadow Over Maplebrook's Tragic Murders?"*

According to the article, a secret group called 'The Keepers of Maplebrook's History' might be behind the recent murders of Professor Emerson and Miranda Clarke. Insiders claimed the group might have seen the victims' actions as a threat to their mission."

"This sounds like something out of a bad mystery novel. A secret society? Really?"

Zoe shrugged, her eyes scanning the room as if expecting a cloak-and-dagger figure to emerge from the shadows. "I know, it's wild. But if it's getting this much attention, there's got to be something we're missing. I'm heading to Palette Whispers. I'll see what gossip I can dig up."

Just then, Sophie Turner breezed into Books and Brew, camera slung over her shoulder and notepad at the ready. "Morning, ladies," she greeted, making a beeline for the counter. "Usual, please."

"Morning, Sophie," I said, pulling an espresso shot with practiced ease. The rich aroma filled the air as I worked the machine, pouring the dark, steaming liquid into her favorite mug.

Next, I selected the plumpest, most inviting blueberry scone from the display, its crumbly exterior promising bursts of tangy sweetness with each bite. I placed both on the counter with a sly smile. I didn't care what she said about watching her figure. I'd seen Sophie eat enough of my scones to know she wouldn't turn one down if present-ed to her. I hoped to entice her to give up some gossip by bribing her with caffeine and carbs. "Here you go, one espresso and your favorite blueberry scone. Warm, just how you like it."

Sophie thanked me. When she started to pull out her wallet, I used it as an opportunity to casually bring up her latest scoop. "Hey, that article about the secret society was a total shocker. I had no idea." I tried to play it cool while handing her the change.

Sophie looked at me with a knowing expression, scone on pause. "It's been quite the talk of the town, hasn't it?" She set down her pastry. "But you know how it is, Piper. A journalist never reveals her sources. It came in an anonymous email, in case you're curious."

I paused, choosing my words carefully. "I am curious, definitely. But it's kinda out there, don't ya think? I have to wonder, though, do you actually believe it?"

For a moment, Sophie appeared to weigh her response before set-ting down her cup with a thoughtful look. "In my line of work, I've learned to keep an open mind. Maplebrook's full of surprises. But honestly, it doesn't matter if I believe it or not. It's all about what the evidence is saying, and right now, it's leaning towards some really interesting theories." She gave me a quick smile and went to sit by the window, leaving me to wonder about her tip and what it meant for our investigation.

Later, after Sophie departed, her words still lingering in the air. Lottie and I set about hanging up the freshly-printed signs for our "Blind Date with a Book" event. The signs, adorned with whimsical fonts and catchy phrases, promised mystery and adventure for anyone brave enough to take a chance on a wrapped book. As we were finishing with the signs, a small group of customers came in, drawn in by the mysteriously-wrapped books at the front. I felt relief to see customers again. Maybe the cloud of Professor Emerson's death was finally lifting.

Lottie, ever the enthusiastic bookseller, jumped at the chance to explain. "So, you pick a book based on the hints we've written on the wrapping. It's a surprise until you get it home and unwrap it!" Her eyes sparkled with excitement. "Who knows, you might just fall in love with a book you'd never have picked up otherwise."

The customers laughed, clearly charmed by the idea. "It's like Tinder for books!" one said, causing a round of giggles to ripple through the group.

"But with less disappointment and ghosting," I added, joining in. "And the worst that can happen is you discover a new author or genre."

As the last of the shoppers filtered out, leaving us in a rare moment of calm, I leaned against the counter, allowing myself a brief pause. I looked at the timeline we had pinned up behind the counter, low enough so no customers could see it. All the evidence, suspects, and unanswered questions were there. That's when it hit me - an image flashed through my mind, unbidden but vivid: I saw Dean Foster walking into Books and Brew with his jacket coated in a fine, distinctive layer of soil, the day after Professor Emerson was found.

I didn't pay much attention to it before, but now it seemed like a big deal. The soil on Dean's jacket was eerily similar to the samples found near Emerson's murder scene, a peculiar type unique to certain areas of Maplebrook—areas like Thornhill's Grove.

"Hey, Lottie," I said, my voice tinged with a newfound urgency. "Do you remember seeing Dean Foster the day after...you know, the first murder?"

Lottie paused, a wrapped book in hand, and furrowed her brow in thought. "Dean? Yeah, he came in for a coffee, looked like he hadn't slept. Why do you ask?"

I chewed on my lip, contemplating the implications. "Just connecting the dots," I mumbled, my mind racing. This new memory could be the key we've been looking for, a solid lead to the killer—or maybe just a fresh angle to investigate.

Later that afternoon, I closed up shop at Books and Brew and locked the door. No one else had come in and the investigation was really getting to me. I hardly ever had to drive in our small town since everything was within walking distance, but today was an exception. I had to be mobile, ready to follow Dean Foster as soon as he left work at the Historical Museum.

My Jeep Wrangler waited for me in the parking lot, its dark blue paint dulled by years of exposure to the elements. The soft top showed signs of fraying, and the bumper had accumulated a few minor scrapes—a testament to our past adventures and my less-than-perfect parallel parking. Just like Maplebrook, the Jeep was both sturdy and full of character.

I hopped into the driver's seat, greeted by the familiar scent of worn leather and a touch of vanilla air freshener. I started the engine, listening to the comforting rumble as it came to life. I took a deep breath, started the car, and headed to the museum.

The museum was quiet, its exhibits and secrets locked away for the night. I parked a bit away, eyes glued to the dark exit, waiting for

Dean to come out. I was so focused on the museum's doors, I nearly jumped out of my skin when a sharp rap on the Jeep's window broke the silence.

My heart raced when I saw Luke's frustrated and concerned expression. His unexpected appearance made me feel really embarrassed because I realized how reckless I must have seemed. Here I was, caught in the act of playing detective in a real-life murder investigation by the one person I was trying to impress with my amateur sleuthing skills.

Luke looked so confident, even in his casual clothes. He was tall and had a solid build, with slightly messy dark hair like he'd running his hands through it. His eyes were a striking shade of green and they showed his seriousness, even though he had a bit of humor in them. He had a charm about him which was intimidating and irresistible, even when he was frustrated.

I could feel myself Books and Brewing when I saw him, even though I tried to play it cool. My heart was racing, not just because of the thrill of almost getting caught, but also because he was so hot. A confusing mix of embarrassment and an unexpected flutter of attraction overcame me, which I wasn't prepared to acknowledge, especially not here and certainly not now. I swallowed, shaking my head. What was wrong with me? I didn't even *like* this guy. Did I?

I rolled down the window, getting ready for the lecture I knew was on its way. "Luke, I-"

"Piper, what are you doing here?" he said, cutting me off. "This isn't safe, and you know it."

He sounded really pissed off, but I knew it was because he cared. I sighed, knowing he was right, but I wasn't ready to give up. "I was just...I thought I might find out something useful," I explained lamely.

"Useful? By tailing people in the dark? Piper, you're not a detective."

"I know, I know," I responded, my resolve wavering under his gaze.

"This isn't a game," Luke's tone softened, his frustration giving way to concern. "It's dangerous."

"It's just—I feel like we're so close, Luke. Dean...there's something off about him. I noticed some of the same dust on his jacket the day after the murder that was found at the crime scene."

Luke's eyebrow went up, letting me know I caught his attention even though he was annoyed. "How would you know about what type of dust was found?

"Um," I said, thinking fast. "I came by to talk to you and saw some notes – test results - on Ruby's desk."

"Ruby left out notes to a murder investigation?" His voice rose exponentially.

I couldn't hurt my friend after all Ruby'd done for me, but I had to convince him my findings were legitimate. "I, well, fished them out from under a bunch of her files."

A thunderstorm took over his expression. Forecast: imminent destruction. "This has got to stop, Piper! Your interference could ruin everything, not to mention buy you a ticket to the morgue. I've got enough deaths on my hands without y—"

I leaned forward, inches from his aquiline nose. "I'm here to help," I interrupted. "My business is on the line, and I feel I'm onto something that might save lives and Maplebrook."

He backed off and ruffled his hair in frustration. Finally, he met my eyes. "How sure are you?"

The distance he'd put between us felt like a chasm. "Pretty sure, anyway. It's something, isn't it?" I pushed, really wanting to convince him I wasn't trying to meddle just to be a pain in his side.

He sighed, deep in thought. "Alright, Piper. I'll check where Dean was when the murders happened. Just promise me you'll stay out of it. Let us handle this. You could get hurt, and I...we can't afford to take that risk."

I nodded, feeling thankful and annoyed at the same time. "Okay, I promise. But you have to keep me updated, Luke. Deal?"

"Deal," he agreed, the tension between us easing slightly. He took my phone from my hand, his fingers brushing against mine, and entered his direct number on speed dial. "Here, call me if you see or hear anything suspicious. Now, go home. And no more late-night stakeouts. Leave the sleuthing to the professionals."

I nodded. "I'm going. Home, I mean," I assured him, but I kept my fingers crossed behind my back. One man couldn't do it all. He needed backup, a sidekick. I couldn't deny the attraction I'd felt being so close to his handsome face.

I waited until his car disappeared around the corner before I started my Jeep again, a mix of guilt and determination churning in my stomach. "Sorry, Luke," I murmured. I couldn't stop until Maplebrook was safe. Romance, I decided, wasn't a part of my life...for now.

Instead of heading home, I drove slowly around the block, giving Luke enough time to clear out before circling back to my original spot near the museum. My heart pounded with a mix of adrenaline and fear. I knew I was pushing my luck, but I was more determined to find the truth and protect my town and my business than scared of getting caught. I settled back in my seat, eyes fixed on the museum's entrance once more, ready to wait out the night if I had to.

The air was heavy with anticipation, with just a flickering streetlamp fighting the darkness. After about fifteen minutes, Dean Foster appeared, his body language tense, constantly glancing over his shoulder like he was looking for someone. He wasn't alone for long. Another figure appeared out of nowhere, moving so smoothly it gave me goosebumps. What in the world was going on?

I strained to discern the details of their clandestine meeting, but they were too far away and their voices were barely audible over the sounds of the rustling leaves in the wind. Under the dim moonlight, I saw their hands meet for a moment, passing something small and unclear—it could've been an object or a pile of papers—from one to the other. My heart raced with excitement and a hint of fear. This was it, the moment of revelation, and I was the sole witness.

I rolled down my window and leaned out as far as could to try to take a picture of the secret meeting. Maybe Luke or someone in the department with mad computer skills could enhance the photo and figure out who Dean was meeting with. All I knew is I was onto something, and whatever Dean was into couldn't be good. I'd deal with the fact that I'd told Luke I was leaving the museum later.

But fate, it seemed, had other plans. A cat chose the moment to leap from a nearby trash can, knocking it over with a loud crash which shattered the evening's silence.

The sudden quiet which followed was almost more shocking than the noise itself. The two figures froze like statues, lit up for a moment by the dim streetlamp. And just as quickly, they vanished into thin air, leaving no trace behind.

I sat there, heart racing, realizing how dangerous things had gotten. I had gone too far alone, and now I could be in the killer's sights.

Great, just what I needed. My big detective moment interrupted by a feline kamikaze mission. As I turned towards the source of the noise, my heart still pounding, I saw a familiar pair of glowing eyes peering at me from the shadows.

"Jazz? Seriously?" I whispered, half in disbelief, half in exasperation. My tuxedo cat, who was supposed to be home enjoying his gourmet rabbit dinner, had apparently decided to follow me on my covert mission. "You nearly gave me a heart attack!"

I scooped him up, feeling the steady rumble of his purrs against my chest. "What are you doing out here, you little troublemaker?" I murmured, feeling a mix of relief and annoyance. "If you're going to be my sidekick, we need to work on your stealth skills."

I carried Jazz to the jeep and loaded him in, making sure he was secure before starting the engine. "Alright, Mr. Purrfect, let's get you back to Books and Brew. We've both had enough excitement for one night."

As I drove back, I couldn't help but reflect on how ridiculous my life had become. "Of all the nights for you to turn into a ninja cat, you pick this one," I said, shaking my head. "Well, at least you saved me from doing something incredibly stupid."

Once we were back inside, I set Jazz down and locked the door behind us. "Let's get you some kibble and me some coffee. We've both had enough excitement for one night."

As I brewed a fresh pot of coffee, I couldn't shake the feeling of being watched. The shadows seemed a little darker, the creaks of the old building a little louder. I knew I needed to be more careful, not just for my sake, but for everyone involved.

But for now, I had a cat to keep safe and a promise to keep to Luke. "Guess I'm staying put for a while, Jazz," I said, scratching behind his ears. "But don't think this means I'm giving up. Just...maybe fewer solo stakeouts. And definitely more backup."

As I settled in with my coffee, I couldn't help but smile at the absurdity of it all. "Here's to you, Jazz," I said, raising my mug. "The best and most unexpected partner a girl could have."

Chapter Seventeen

♥

The morning light filtered through the sheer curtains of my loft, gently nudging me awake. Jazz, nestled under the warm covers, provided a comforting weight on my feet, his purring making it hard to get out of bed. I sighed reluctantly and pulled my feet out from under him, prompting a sleepy meow of protest as he stretched out and took over the warm space.

After attending to Jazz's breakfast, which included a mix of his preferred kibble and a small amount of canned food for an indulgence, I made my way to the bathroom to start getting ready for the day. I decided on comfort and functionality, donning dark jeans, a comfortable graphic print tee featuring a stack of books with the phrase "Book Nerd" emblazoned across it, and my dependable Converse shoes. No fashion vibes today. I tied my hair in a loose ponytail and remembered to grab the Jeep keys. The blue Wrangler, which had been super busy lately, was perfect for sneaking around - like going to last night's secret meeting spot.

Ready to go, I quickly grabbed my purse, keys, and phone. Jazz, done with breakfast, followed me with curious eyes as I double-checked myself in the mirror. "Don't wait up," I joked, knowing full well he'd likely spend the day napping in sunbeams until my return.

Leaving my loft and ensuring the door was securely locked, a surge of both excitement and anxiety washed over me. I knew the day would bring more questions, but I was determined to find answers. The Jeep, parked just outside, its blue paint job a bit dull from the dust of last night's reconnaissance, seemed almost to beckon, promising a lead in the right direction.

As I headed towards the Jeep, I briefly considered the idea of back-up. I had mentioned it to Luke last night, but I didn't have time to coordinate with anyone this morning. Besides, I reasoned, this was just a quick follow-up. Nothing dangerous, right? Plus, waiting around for someone to join me would only slow things down. I needed to keep moving.

"Alright, Piper," I muttered to myself as I climbed into the driver's seat, "you've got this." With a deep breath, I started the engine and set off for the Historical Museum, the determination to uncover the truth driving me forward.

I wasn't sure what I was looking for this early in the morning, but I felt like I needed to go back and check things out in the daylight. Surely things wouldn't look as ominous as they had in the dark shadows last night. I parked and hopped out of the Jeep, scanning the area. I was right; it felt different in the sunshine.

I walked up to the exact location where I had observed Dean and the other man engaging in their covert meeting. The sound of rustling leaves accompanied my footsteps, while the cheerful chirping of birds in the morning added an uneasy edge to my feelings.

And that's when I spotted it. Underneath a bush, there was a piece of paper, barely visible. I carefully reached down and picked it up, feeling the cool, damp earth. It was a copy of an old land deed, the edges slightly crumpled, but the writing clear. Annotated in the margins were notes which hinted at a secret amendment related to the land surrounding Thornhill's Grove.

As I unfolded the paper fully, the annotations came into sharper focus, suggesting a manipulative scheme which tied directly back to the heart of the mystery. It wasn't just about land or money; it was all about power, control, and how far someone would go to protect their interests.

With the document in hand, I knew I had to be cautious. This was some serious evidence that could expose all the lies in our town.

"Piper, what are you doing here so early?"

Startled, I spun around, my heart racing as the document almost slipped from my hands. "Dean! You scared me," I stammered, hastily stuffing the paper into my bag. "Just...out for a morning walk. You know, trying to clear my head."

He raised an eyebrow, his gaze drifting to my bag. "A walk, huh? With a Jeep parked right there?" His tone was light, but I knew he wasn't buying it.

Nervously, I let out a small chuckle, attempting to steer the conversation in a different direction. "Yeah, well, you never know when you'll need to make a quick getaway from all this...peace and tranquility."

The sound of Dean's laughter helped to alleviate the tension. "Fair enough. I was actually here to talk to a local botanist about the development plans near Thornhill's Grove. Trying to see if we can stop it without causing too much drama."

"Oh?" I perked up, genuinely interested. "And how's that going?"

He sighed, rubbing the back of his neck. "It's complicated. The proposed development could really damage the ecosystem around the Grove. We're looking into the environmental impacts, hoping to gather enough evidence to present a case against it."

I nodded, impressed by his dedication. "That sounds really important. I didn't realize you were involved in something like that." I thought about the land deed and shook my head. I had so many questions, but still wasn't sure who I could trust. "Did the Professor know about the ecological impact to the area?"

Dean paused, considering his answer. "Yes, he did. Professor Emerson was actually quite supportive of our efforts to protect it. He believed the historical significance of Thornhill's Grove was just as crucial as its environmental value. He was helping us compile historical evidence to bolster our case against the development."

It all suddenly made sense in my head. "So, his research wasn't just academic; it had a real-world application that could have stopped the development?"

"Exactly," Dean affirmed. "Anyway, what about you? What brings you out here, really? It can't just be for a walk."

Dean's question caught me off-guard, so I took a moment to decide. I didn't really know if I could trust him with everything I found out. "Oh, you know, just needed some fresh air. Clear my head a bit," I managed, hoping my casual tone would mask my real intentions.

As Dean nodded, albeit somewhat unconvinced.

"Well, I should probably head off. Got a lot to think about," I said, making my way back to my Wrangler, the document safely tucked away in my bag.

But as luck would have it, my Wrangler chose that moment to betray me. The engine was being a pain and wouldn't start, no matter how much I begged and prodded the ignition. Feeling frustrated and a little panicked, I was weighing my options when someone knocked on the window and made me jump.

Turning, I saw Ethan, the town's philanthropist's expression one of mild concern. "Everything alright? That doesn't sound too good," he said, nodding towards the uncooperative engine.

Wearing jeans and a worn jacket, he stood there with his hands in his pockets in the chilly morning air. His tousled sandy hair gave the impression he had been running his fingers through it, either in frustration or deep thought. I briefly wondered why Ethan was here at this hour, of all people. Was it mere coincidence, or was there a reason he appeared just when I found myself stranded?

"Yes, car trouble," I said, my mind racing with the implications of his sudden appearance. "I, um, didn't expect to see anyone else out here so early."

A trace of worry or maybe even deliberate calculation appeared on Ethan's brow. "I was just on my way to check on a few things at one of the development sites. Saw you struggling with your car and thought I'd offer some help," he explained, his tone friendly but holding an edge I couldn't quite place.

Caught off-guard, I still managed a little smile. "Yeah, my car's acting up. I was about to call for a tow."

Ethan shook his head. "No need for that. I can give you a lift. Where do you need to go?"

I considered his offer. I had a feeling it was a bad idea, but then again, could be an opportunity. "Actually, I was headed to the police station. To see Luke. Got some paperwork to discuss," I ventured, hoping the mention of the police would serve as a subtle reminder my whereabouts were accounted for.

Ethan simply nodded, gesturing for me to join him. "Sure thing. Let's get you there."

As we settled into the car, the interior was neat, the air filled with the faint scent of leather and something else I couldn't quite place. "Thanks for this, Ethan."

Ethan started the engine, a rumble beneath the hood betraying the car's age. "No problem at all. Always happy to help out a neighbor. Plus, it lets me take a break from all the real estate craziness," he said, smoothly getting on the road.

I tried to play it casual. "You mentioned you were checking out your development stuff. What new things do you have on the horizon?"

"Oh, you know, just the usual," he responded with a casual confidence which comes from years of experience in real estate development. Expanding some residential areas, looking into revitalizing some of the older parts of town. Maplebrook's growing, and we need to grow with it," he explained, keeping his eyes on the road.

I nodded, trying to match his tone while my mind raced. It was a weird conversation, like we were just skirting around what really mattered. "That sounds ambitious. Must be a lot to manage, especially with all the environmental regulations and such."

The sound of Ethan's chuckle didn't match the tension I felt; it was too laid-back. "Ah, yes, the joys of paperwork and permits. But it's all part of the job. Keeps things interesting."

It was then, as I glanced down to adjust my seatbelt, that I saw it. Ethan's shoes were covered in light, powdery dust, just like the kind found at Thornhill's Grove and the murder scenes.

Chapter Eighteen

♥

E than's voice was calm, almost soothing, a stark contrast to the tension that coiled tight in my stomach. "You know, Piper, Maplebrook is a town of secrets," he began, his eyes on the road. "Some secrets are buried deep, others tend to surface when you least expect them."

I kept a straight face, gripping the door handle a little tighter to make it seem like I was just bracing myself. "Secrets? In Maplebrook?" I feigned a light laugh. "I thought our biggest secret was Mrs. Jenkins' pie recipe."

He chuckled, but his eyes didn't seem to agree. "Ah, but some secrets have far greater consequences. Like the truth behind certain ...research projects," he said, giving me a quick glance before turning his attention back to the road.

This was it. He was talking about the murders, about Professor Emerson and Miranda. But I had to be careful, play dumb until I could figure a way out of this. "Research projects? I suppose there's always something going on in the academic world. Nothing that would interest a simple bookstore owner like me."

Ethan's smile didn't waver, but the air grew colder. "Don't sell yourself short, Piper. You've shown quite the knack for uncovering hidden truths. It would be a shame if that curiosity led you...astray."

It was obvious the warning was a threat disguised as friendly advice. My mind was racing, trying to figure out how to escape or get help. But for now, I had to keep him chatting, pretending I didn't grasp the seriousness of what he was implying.

The car came to a halt and I immediately noticed a drastic change in the surroundings. We left the vibrant streets of Maplebrook behind and entered the tranquil woods that surrounded Thornhill's Grove. My pulse started racing; this was not where I expected Ethan would bring me.

He switched off the motor and directed his serious gaze towards me. "Piper, I brought you here to show you the future of Maplebrook. The development around Thornhill's Grove will bring prosperity to our town, something I've worked tirelessly to achieve."

I forced myself to swallow, attempting to stay composed. "And the Professor? And Miranda? Did they disagree with this future?"

Ethan's gaze hardened. "They saw things differently, yes. But sometimes, to build a better future, obstacles must be removed. It's not personal, Piper. It's business."

My heart sank. There it was, a confession wrapped in justification. He had killed them to protect his interests, and now, here I was, alone with him, potentially the next obstacle in his path.

"But why me, Ethan? Why bring me here?" My voice was steady, but inside, I was screaming for a way out.

He sighed, a hint of regret in his eyes. "You're smart, Piper. You've pieced together more than anyone else. I respect that. But it also makes you dangerous to my plans. I hoped I could convince you to see things my way."

A bitter laugh escaped my lips. This guy was seriously crazy. "And if I don't?"

With his jaw clenched, Ethan averted his gaze. "Then I'm afraid you leave me no choice but to ensure you can't interfere any further."

A surge of panic coursed through my veins, my heart pounding in my chest as I clenched my fists, desperate to conceal the terror I felt. I needed a plan, and fast. "Ethan, you don't have to do this. Think of the consequences."

He responded with a grim smile. "I've thought of nothing else, Piper. But I've come too far to turn back now."

His sudden movement caught me off guard. A swift, hard motion aimed directly at my head. I moved on instinct, but not quick enough to avoid contact completely. The world spun, pain exploded, but the thick scrunchie in my hair softened the blow, keeping the darkness at bay.

He probably thought I was out cold because the next thing I knew, I was getting shuffled around. Ethan grabbed me and put me in the back seat of his car. The door closed with a thud, sealing me inside.

The engine started, sounding like a muffled rumble in my confusion. Then, a faint whiff of exhaust fumes began to fill the area. My brain was foggy, but the surge of panic sliced through the haze with intensity. Ethan was trying to kill me, quietly, invisibly, with carbon monoxide.

With sheer determination, I battled the darkness and kept my eyes open. All I cared about was staying alive. My arms and legs were like bricks, but I pushed through, fueled by desperation. I went to open the door, but someone had taken off the locks on purpose.

Panic flirted with the edges of my thoughts, a relentless suitor in this deadly dance. "Great, Piper, locked in a car like a bad 'nineties thriller. What next, signaling Morse code with the dome light?" I muttered to myself, the absurdity of my situation momentarily lightening the dread. My gaze landed on the windows, the only barrier between me and precious, life-giving air. "Guess it's time to reenact my own escape room challenge. Minus the helpful clues and cheerful end-game buzzer." With each kick, I half-expected canned audience applause or a disembodied voice saying, "Congratulations, you've found the exit. Please collect your belongings and ego on the way out."

My foot connected with the passenger side window once more, a mix of frustration and panic. "Come on, Piper, think!" I chided myself internally, regretting not piecing the clues together sooner. The thought of leaving Jazz behind, my loyal companion through thick and thin, spurred a fresh wave of determination. "I can't let him down," I thought, as I prepared for another attempt, driven by the thought of my furry friend waiting at home.

I promised I'd bring Jazz all the treats he wanted if I could get out of this death trap. Kicking again with all the force I could muster, I finally saw a small crack in the window. Relief sunk in, and I kicked again, over and over, until finally, the window shattered.

The window crack was like a glimmer of hope. "Treats for a year, Jazz," I pledged into the heavy air, each word punctuated with a kick. Fueled by determination, my foot relentlessly pounded against the glass. And then, the sweetest sound—glass giving way. Relief washed over me. "Hold on, Jazz, I'm coming back," I whispered, clawing my way through the shattered window, the promise of fresh air driving me forward with a fervor I hadn't known I possessed.

After regaining my breath, I quickly glanced around, trying to figure out where I was. My gaze fell on my purse, unceremoniously dumped beside the car, now decorated with a fine layer of dust and dirt. "Oh, great, just great," I muttered, half-amused, half-irritated. "Not the Kate Spade, Zoe will kill me if she sees this." I picked it up, brushing it off with more care than I had for my own well-being. "Survive a murder attempt? Sure. Ruin a perfectly good handbag? Unforgivable." Priorities, after all.

I glanced up to see Ethan pacing near the edge of the development site. "What's he doing now?" I muttered to myself, suspicion knotting in my stomach. Was he looking for something, or was this a victory lap of sorts? Shaking the thoughts away, I realized this might be my only chance.

I quickly grabbed my phone from the purse. "Okay, Ethan, let's see how you like being overheard," I whispered, my voice laced with a mix of fear and determination. I speed-dialed Luke's number, slipping the phone back into my pocket, the call ongoing. My breath hitched as I waited, praying he would pick up and understand the silent message I was desperately trying to send.

Steeling my nerves, I stepped closer to Ethan, who turned at the sound of my approach, surprise flickering across his face before it settled into a smirk. "Piper, what a surprise. I was under the impression you had a more stationary evening planned."

"Yeah, well, you know me, always popping up where I'm least expected," I shot back, trying to keep my voice steady. "Like daisies in a lawn—persistent and hard to get rid of."

Ethan chuckled, a sound that sent shivers down my spine. "Daisies, huh? I always took you for more of a thorn in my side."

"Speaking of thorns," I said, edging closer to the heart of Thornhill's Grove. "Let's talk about your latest gardening project. Seems to me you've been planting more than just flowers. More like lies and deceit? You owe me that much after *you tried to kill me,*" I said with emphasis, hoping Luke was getting every word.

His expression darkened, the facade slipping as he realized I was onto him. "You really have no idea what you're meddling with, do you? This—this is about legacy, Piper. About ensuring this town grows and thrives, even if it means making hard decisions."

"Hard decisions?" I echoed, incredulous. "Is that what we're calling murder these days? Because I'm pretty sure the last time I checked, 'thinning out the competition' didn't involve actual thinning of people."

Ethan's composure wavered, a flicker of anger in his eyes. "You think you understand, but you don't. This town, my family's role in it—it's bigger than you or any single life."

I couldn't help but snort. "Wow, Ethan, and here I thought my biggest problem today was going to be choosing between latte flavors. Turns out, it's actually dodging the philosophical musings of a murderer."

He glared at me to stop, but I was on a roll. "Protecting your legacy, huh? That's a fancy way of saying 'murdering for profit,' isn't it, Ethan?" I taunted, keeping my voice light but my stance ready for anything. Ethan's casual demeanor faltered for a moment, a flicker of something darker crossing his face.

"Legacy is what lasts, Piper," he said, his tone chillingly calm. "It's what we leave behind. And sometimes, protecting that requires drastic measures."

"Oh, I get it. Like a 'murder mystery with real stakes' kind of drastic?" I tried to keep him talking, aware every word might be pouring into Luke's attentive ears.

Ethan's eyes narrowed, and for a moment, he just stared at me, assessing. Then, his gaze dropped to my pocket, and his expression changed. "You think you're clever, recording this? You think you'll get away with this, Piper?"

Before I could react, he lunged at me, his hand reaching for my pocket. My heart leaped into my throat as I darted back, trying to put distance between us. "Nice try, but you'll have to be faster than that!" I exclaimed, though my voice betrayed the fear starting to take hold. To my surprise, he'd loosened the phone from my pocket.

As it skidded across the gravel, coming to a stop precariously close to a shallow pit left by the development's excavation, my heart raced. Ethan's sudden lunge for the device seemed almost in slow motion, yet I knew my window of opportunity was rapidly closing.

"Looking for this?" I taunted, surprising even myself with the steadiness of my voice as I stepped towards the phone. His eyes darted from me to the phone, calculating, his posture tensed for another attack.

But I wasn't about to let him have the upper hand. I mustered all my courage and made a split-second choice. "You know, for a man with such grand plans for this town, you sure don't mind getting your hands dirty," I said, aiming to keep him talking to buy time.

His only response was a growl of frustration, his gaze fixed on me with an intensity that sent shivers down my spine. Just as he was about to act, I sprinted to the phone, my heart thumping in my ears.

Just as my fingers brushed against the cold metal, Ethan's hand closed around my wrist, his grip iron-tight. Panic flared within me, but I refused to let it show. "Let go of me. You won't get away with this," I said, struggling against his hold.

But then, something unexpected happened. Suddenly, the gravel beneath Ethan's feet shifted—the same loose patch where Zoe had done her impression of Bambi on ice the other evening. He wavered, and for a split second, it seemed like he might actually regain his balance. But no, gravity had other plans. With a surprised yelp, he tumbled backward into the shallow pit, letting go of me in the process. The sudden loss of his grip sent me flailing, and I fell backward, landing hard on the gravel-strewn ground. Classic, Piper, I thought. Just another day in the life.

Chapter Nineteen

♥

My head throbbed as I slowly sat up, realizing my new white Converse were now covered with dirt. "Seriously? These were brand new!" I groaned, wincing at the pain radiating through my skull. I brushed off my cute jeans, trying to shake off the dirt and the frustration. "Great, now I need a new pair of shoes and a chiropractor." I glanced down at Ethan's prone form and sighed. Jazz would never let me live this down; I owed him a truckload of treats for getting me through this—*if* I got through this.

The sound of approaching cars cut through the silence, and I squinted into the distance. I watched as headlights pierced through the morning fog, praying it was a convoy of salvation. "Showtime," I whispered, praying for the cavalry's arrival.

The first to jump out was, to my utter surprise, Sophie. Behind her, Luke, Zoe, and Lottie with a a mix of concern and determination on their faces.

Sophie, camera and notepad at the ready as if prepared to conduct an impromptu press conference right there in the gravel, had a look of sheer determination which mirrored the urgency of the situation. Her usual reporter's instinct to chase the story was tempered by a genuine concern for my wellbeing, a surprising but welcome layer to her character I hadn't fully appreciated before.

Luke, meanwhile, wasn't alone. Beside him stood two other officers, their expressions stern and focused, clearly prepared for whatever might unfold. They had come ready to back up Luke.

"Looks like I dialed the wrong number, but it turned out to be the right mistake," I said, pushing myself to a stand with effort.

Sophie raised an eyebrow, a slight smirk on her lips. "You owe me one, Piper. Who knew my nosiness would come in handy?"

Luke was next to me in an instant, his professional concern taking over. "Are you okay? What happened?"

"I meant to call you, Luke," I explained, still catching my breath. "But I accidentally dialed Sophie's number instead. Turns out it was a lucky mistake."

Luke nodded, glancing at Sophie. "Good thing she did. Sophie called me right after you hung up and told me where you were. We got here as fast as we could."

Sophie nodded, her smirk turning into a genuine smile. "Always happy to help, especially when it's this exciting."

Luke gave a quick nod of appreciation to Sophie before turning back to me. "Good thing she picked up. Now, tell me everything that happened."

I waved him off, still trying to maintain a bit of humor. "Oh, you know, just a typical day. Got into a bit of a scuffle with the local villain. But don't worry, my secret weapon was a hair tie. High-quality stuff."

"And here I thought the biggest danger in Maplebrook was stale scones," Zoe interjected. She peeked down into the shallow hole. "Ethan? I *knew* it!"

"Stale scones might still be a close second," I managed to say with a weak smile, grateful for Zoe's light-hearted spirit even in the midst of danger. "Turns out, Ethan was more interested in land grabs than real estate ethics."

I reached into my purse to pull out the copy of the land deed—but it wasn't there. Panic rose as the realization hit me. I gasped, feeling a cold wave of dismay wash over me. "Ethan must have taken it when I was out of it." I looked up, meeting the concerned glances of my friends. "That was our smoking gun. It linked him directly to the murders, all for his twisted development plans."

As Luke dragged Ethan out of the pit, securing handcuffs around his wrists, I called followed him. "Luke, check his jacket. He took something from me." Ethan was stirring, consciousness creeping back into his expression, but Luke nodded, understanding the urgency in my voice.

He patted down Ethan's jacket and, sure enough, pulled out the folded copy of the deed. "This what you were looking for?" he asked, holding it up for me to see.

Relief washed over me. "That's it. The missing piece." I held up the paper. "This document shows that the original deed was amended, letting Ethan commercially develop Thornhill's Grove. But the Professor's research revealed the land was historically and environmentally significant. His findings would have invalidated the amendment, exposing Ethan's manipulations and protecting the land. That's why he had to silence the professor."

Luke raised an eyebrow, clearly interested. "Historically and environmentally significant? How so?"

I took a deep breath, diving into the explanation. "Okay, so Thornhill's Grove sits on top of this rich tungsten deposit. This stuff is like gold for industrial applications and could bring a lot of money to Maplebrook if mined properly. But here's the kicker—developing the site would mean disturbing Eliza Maplebrook's grave and potentially wrecking the town's historical roots. Eliza, the wife of the town's founder, is buried there. Her grave is a local landmark. Plus, the grove is where the town was originally founded. Professor Emerson's research showed all this, making it clear the area needed to be preserved."

Luke's eyes widened as the full picture came into view. "So Ethan wanted to develop the land for the tungsten, but Emerson's research would have stopped him?"

"Exactly," I said, holding up the document. "The amendment to the deed was made to allow commercial development, but if the land's significance was proven, that amendment would be invalidated. Ethan stood to gain a lot from the tungsten, but he couldn't do it without silencing anyone who got in his way."

Sophie, who had been listening intently, nodded in understanding. "So, Ethan manipulated the deed and then tried to cover his tracks by getting rid of anyone who could expose him, including Professor Emerson."

"Yes," I confirmed. "And now we have the proof we need to show his true intentions."

Luke looked at the paper, then back at me. "This is huge, Piper. We can finally bring Ethan to justice."

"Right," Zoe jumped in. "Dean mentioned he saw Miranda arguing with someone just days before her murder. We all thought it pointed to Dean, but now it's clear—it must have been Ethan she confronted. Maybe she found out about his plans and threatened to expose him."

I nodded. "Remember the petition we found Miranda spearheaded, advocating for a major development project right next to Thornhill's Grove? It's clear she found out about the professor's research and had a change of heart to avoid the area. That's why she didn't want him to go public—she knew it would back Ethan into a corner."

"Then Ethan decided to eliminate her, too," said Lottie. "It fits with the pattern of silencing anyone who posed a threat to his development project."

"Looks like our local real estate mogul/philanthropist had a side hustle in creative writing," Sophie said, rolling her eyes. "Those anonymous tips had Ethan written all over them. Guess he figured he could steer the narrative. Too bad for him that he's not the only one with a knack for uncovering the truth."

"Turns out his plot had more holes than the mystery novels Piper sells at Books and Brew," Zoe added.

"At least we know Maplebrook's real estate market is booming," Lottie chimed in, ever the optimist. "Too bad Ethan's next development will be behind bars."

Even Luke, usually the most serious of the bunch, couldn't help but crack a smile. "I have to admit, this was one case I'm glad to close with all of you. Though, Piper, next time, maybe stick to recommending books instead of chasing criminals."

I laughed, feeling the tension finally begin to lift. "Deal, but only if you promise to stock up on detective novels. It seems we have quite the knack for solving mysteries—maybe it's our new calling."

"Just make sure you dial the right number next time, Piper," Sophie said, seizing the moment for one last jab. "Though, I must say, accidentally calling the local gossip queen turned out to be the best mistake you ever made."

"I'd have to agree," I said, for once, thankful for her pushiness.

"Wait a minute," Zoe started. "Who left you the note the day of the professor's lecture? Surely *that* wasn't Ethan."

I shook my head. It was still one piece of the puzzle I hadn't been able to quite make fit. "I have to think it was Professor Emerson."

"That makes sense," Lottie said. "Maybe he wanted to make sure someone would keep digging if...well, if anything happened to him."

The pieces finally fell into place. "He must've known he was onto something big, something dangerous. And with the lecture at Books and Brew, who better to leave a clue for than the owner?"

Zoe raised an eyebrow, the gears turning in her head. "So, in a way, we were his backup plan. The Professor trusted you, Piper, even if he never said it outright."

I let out a soft laugh, touched by the notion. "The Murder Mystery Book Club: the Professor's last resort. He really must've been desperate."

Lottie's laughter filled the air, lightening the mood. "Well, I say we did him proud."

"What about the note detailing the meetings between Charlie and the Professor about his discoveries at Thornhill's Grove?" Zoe asked. "The Professor did not leave that anonymous note."

"I think it was Miranda," I said, feeling one more piece click into place. "She was trying to tip someone off about the property's significance without exposing herself." I pondered a little bit more. "Ethan must have known she had the document. That's probably what they were arguing about." I couldn't help it, I kept connecting more dots. "Ethan saw her as a threat to his secret being exposed. It all starts to make a twisted kind of sense."

Ethan, now fully conscious and handcuffed, glared at us, his earlier composure replaced by a simmering rage. "Your community's little investigation club might have outsmarted me this time," Ethan spat, trying to keep his voice steady.

"I wouldn't plan on there being a next time," Luke advised gruffly, leading him toward the police vehicle. I plan to look into all of your real estate dealings.

Zoe couldn't help herself. "Looks like Maplebrook's got its own brand of justice, huh? Maybe next time, don't mess with book lovers and their town."

"It was all Piper," Lottie added softly. "She figured it out."

I shrugged, feeling a mix of relief and exhaustion. "I just didn't want to see our town's history or its future compromised. And I couldn't have done it without all of you."

As Luke led Ethan away, he turned back to us. "Piper, you and your... 'Murder Mystery Book Club,' was it?" He chuckled lightly, the tension in his shoulders easing. "You've done something remarkable here."

I felt a flush of pride but played it cool. "We do have a knack for stirring things up." I shared a glance with Zoe and Lottie, who beamed back at me.

Luke's expression softened further, a smile creeping in. "It's more than that. Your connection to this community, your persistence—it made a difference. This was a team effort, and I—I'm grateful for your help."

Sophie, ever ready to capture the moment, raised her camera. "This sounds like the beginning of a beautiful partnership," she said, a twinkle in her eye.

Luke nodded before turning back to Ethan. "Just don't make this a habit, alright? My heart can't take the excitement."

I nodded, knowing full well if another mystery came knocking, I'd probably dive headfirst into it again. But for now, Ethan's murders had been stopped, and Maplebrook could breathe a little easier.

"As for the festival," Sophie chimed in, ever the journalist looking for a silver lining. "I think this whole ordeal will make one heck of a story. 'Small Town Solves Its Own Murder Mystery.' How's that for a headline?"

Chapter Twenty

♥

The shop was buzzing with activity, a complete turnaround from the tense atmosphere a few days ago. As I got behind the counter, pouring coffee and sharing smiles, I couldn't help but feel the cozy vibe at Books and Brew. The rich aroma of coffee and pastries created a warm and welcoming environment. Laughter filled the room, accompanied by the sounds of cups clinking and pages turning. The entire community found comfort in our cozy bookstore café, as if we were the heart of it all.

It felt like a tremendous relief, not just for me, but for everyone in Maplebrook. I rewarded myself with not just one—but two —snickerdoodles, and didn't feel the least bit guilty. I gave Jazz his promised treats, and he thanked me by showing me his belly and purring incessantly.

As I enjoyed the sweet, crunchy cookies, Zoe leaned in, giving the cookies a playful look. "Two snickerdoodles? Really setting the bar high for celebratory snacks, aren't we?"

I grinned, wiping away a crumb. "After what we've been through, I think I've earned a whole batch. Besides, Jazz agreed with me, didn't you, buddy?"

Jazz, the ultimate opportunist when it came to treats, remained blissfully unaware of our conversation, his purring providing moral support in its own unique way.

Without skipping a beat, Lottie gracefully moved in between tables. "If we decide to treat ourselves with cookies, I'm calling dibs on the chocolate chip ones. I think my detective work was at least worth five of those."

"Five?" Zoe raised an eyebrow, her playful tone evident. "Why settle for stopping there? Let's indulge in a whole day of celebrating our sleuthing skills, surrounded by an endless buffet of Evie's mouthwatering treats."

I couldn't help but laugh, feeling the warmth of their company and the café's buzzing ambiance. "I think we might be onto something here. 'Detectives' Day Out: All the Cookies You Can Investigate.' We could even make it an annual event at Books and Brew."

"Count me in on that," Lottie said with a laugh.

The atmosphere in the cafe became electric as the evening went on. Customers came and went, all headed towards the town square for the festival's closing gala. Lots of people stopped to chat about the case, curious about the crazy drama. They congratulated us and wanted all the details about our 'detective' work.

Zoe, with her natural talent for storytelling, kept everyone entertained with exaggerated tales of our adventures, making us laugh and gasp at the same time. Her stories really brought our journey to life and got everyone excited for the gala.

On the flip side, Lottie was all about practicality - she made sure everyone had a full cup of coffee and fresh pastries, while also sneaking in her witty observations about what had happened. "You know," she'd say, handing over a latte with a smile. "It turns out solving murders requires a lot of caffeine. Who knew?"

I found myself alternating between assisting and participating in conversations, feeling the comforting embrace of community. It was in those moments, hanging out with friends and neighbors, when I realized how Books and Brew and the Murder Mystery Book Club had become so important to Maplebrook's community.

"This place is jammed," I commented to Zoe during a rare quiet moment behind the counter.

With a grin, she leaned against the espresso machine. "Seems like we're not just your average book club anymore. We're local celebrities now."

"Speaking of celebrities, I came to get my first-hand interview." Sophie's arrival was marked by her characteristic flair, notebook poised as if she were about to break the next big story. "So, Piper, ready to spill the beans to your favorite journalist?" she asked, the tease in her voice not quite masking a professional edge. "Who knew you had detective skills up your sleeve? Any thoughts on making it official?"

I raised my eyebrow with a mix of humor and skepticism. "Coffee and books are my thing for now, Sophie. Less chance of getting kidnapped or worse. But thanks for the vote of confidence."

Just as Sophie was about to reply, my mother and Ruby showed up, filling the room with laughter and playful teasing. Margie, always finding a romantic angle, gave me a knowing look and nudged me. "I always said there's nothing like a little adventure to spark a romance, Dear. Any handsome detectives catching your eye lately?"

I rolled my eyes, the fond irritation ready to surface in my voice. "Mom, can we not turn my near-death experience into a matchmaking opportunity? Let's just focus on celebrating the festival and forgetting about murderers for a while."

Margie was not one to take a hint. "Luke is quite the catch. And now that the case is closed--"

Before she could finish, Ruby chimed in, nodding in agreement. "Oh, absolutely. And I heard his divorce is final. He could use a good woman by his side."

I couldn't help but argue, although a small part of me couldn't deny Luke's appeal. "Mom, Ruby, can we not do this right now? I've had enough excitement to last a lifetime. Besides, Luke and I are just colleagues."

"But Piper," Margie persisted. "You two make such a great team! And after everything you've been through, it's clear you have a special connection."

"Let's focus on the festival and Books and Brew, okay? I added quickly, trying to steer the conversation away. "Not my—our non-existent love lives."

Ruby, sensing my discomfort sighed. "Just think about it," she pushed gently. It's not every day you find someone who understands the dangers and thrills of chasing down a mystery. Luke gets that part of you."

I groaned softly, feeling the weight of their expectations but also a curious flutter at the thought of Luke. "Let's just say I'll consider it—after the festival. Right now, I think the only partnership I'm ready for is with my bed and a long sleep."

Margie and Ruby exchanged knowing glances, their matchmaking schemes momentarily paused but clearly not forgotten. "Alright," my mom conceded with a smile. "But don't think we're giving up on this. Maplebrook could use a little more romance, after all."

"Plus, he's *hot*," Zoe threw in, making the conversation take an unexpected turn. Her flair for stirring the pot drew a round of laughter, even from me. I just prayed Luke wouldn't get wind of our discussion.

Sophie, ever the opportunist, snapped her notebook shut with a decisive click. "Well, if you're not interested, sounds like he's fair game." She sauntered towards the door, leaving a trail of intrigue in her wake.

Her comment did something to me, sparking a flame of possessiveness I hadn't realized was there. But before I could dissect the new swirl of emotions, the door swung open, and in walked Luke, the man of the hour.

His entrance was less the law enforcement officer I'd come to know and more the charming Maplebrook local I'd only glimpsed in passing moments. He wore a soft, heather-gray Henley that complemented his lean build, paired with faded jeans which spoke of comfort rather than duty. The absence of his detective's badge and the casual roll of his sleeves revealed an ease I hadn't seen in him before. His smile, warm and unrestrained, seemed to brighten the already-lively Books and Brew even further.

As he approached, I felt a flutter of something unexpected—a mix of anticipation and nervousness. His casual appearance threw me off balance, showcasing a side of Luke which was undeniably attractive and disarmingly human. It was a reminder that beyond the cases and the clues, there was a man who had stepped into the fray beside us, not just as a detective, but as a friend and perhaps something more. The realization caught me off guard, stirring a curiosity about what lay beneath the surface of our burgeoning friendship.

"Congratulations, Piper, and to the whole Murder Mystery Book Club," he said, his tone warm but carrying the ever-present hint of authority. "You've done Maplebrook proud."

Lottie, unable to resist, stepped in. "Hear that, Piper? You've done Maplebrook proud. Now, if only you could solve the mystery of how to get you two on a date." Her wink was as mischievous as it was teasing.

I shot her a look, part exasperation, part amusement. "Lottie, I swear, your matchmaking is more relentless than Sophie's journalism."

Luke chuckled, clearly amused by our banter. "Well, I'll leave you to it. Just wanted to say well done. And, Piper," he paused, meeting my eyes. "We make a good team." There was something in his gaze, a promise or perhaps a challenge, which made my heart skip a beat.

"Thanks, Luke," I managed, my voice steadier than I felt. "And who knows? Maybe there are more mysteries for us to solve together."

As he nodded and turned to leave, the room buzzed with the possibilities of what lay ahead. Sophie, seizing the moment for one last jab, called after him. "Just so you know, Piper, you've got some competition."

My immediate roll of the eyes was more reflexive than I cared to admit. "Didn't she hear me say I wasn't interested in dating? Luke or anyone else?" But even as I spoke, the seed of doubt Sophie planted nagged at me, mingling with the curiosity Luke's new look had sparked.

Lottie, rummaging through a stack of unopened mail by the register, paused and waved an envelope in the air. "Hey, Piper, this looks fancy," she said, a curious lilt in her voice.

I walked over, wiping my hands on my apron. "What's that?" I asked, taking the envelope from her. It was heavier than usual, with a sophisticated wax seal on the back, embossed with an intricate mermaid emblem. My name was written in elegant script across the front.

"Looks like an invitation," Zoe chimed in, peering over my shoulder as I carefully broke the seal and unfolded the paper inside.

"Dear Piper Page," I read aloud. "You are cordially invited to the grand opening weekend at The Muddy Mermaid, a sanctuary for those seeking relaxation and rejuvenation in our serene environment."

My eyebrows shot up. "The Muddy Mermaid? That's the new high-end spa and retreat on Willow Lane, isn't it?" I glanced at Zoe and Lottie, a mixture of surprise and intrigue on my face.

"It's not cheap to stay there," Lottie added, her interest piqued. "What did you do to get an invite to something like that?"

"I have no idea," I admitted, scanning the rest of the invitation. "But it mentions their grand opening weekend. Maybe they're trying to attract locals to spread the word?" I honestly had no idea why I'd receive such an invite, but a free weekend at a high-end spa wasn't something I was about to pass up, especially after the last few days.

Slipping the invitation into my bag, I momentarily forgot about it, my mind now focused on the evening ahead. "Let's go show Maplebrook how to celebrate a mystery solved, shall we?" I followed everyone out, locking up Books and Brew.

"First order of business at the gala: find the dessert table," Zoe declared, her priorities always in the right place.

"And avoid any matchmaking schemes," I added, shooting a glance at Lottie, who held up her hands in mock surrender. "After all this, you deserve a bit of fun. And if that includes a handsome detective or two, who am I to argue?"

Laughing, we made our way to the town square, the gala lights beckoning us forward. For tonight, at least, we could forget about mysteries, murderers, and matchmaking and just enjoy being together, celebrating our victory and the community we loved.

The future could wait. For now, the Murder Mystery Book Club was off duty, ready to dance the night away under the stars.

The End

Keep reading for the next book in the series, Mud, Masks, and Murder: A Piper Page Cozy Mystery Book 2

About the Author

❤

Lucy Penbrook is embarking on her first foray into cozy mystery writing with her Piper Page Cozy Mystery Series. Although new to the cozy mystery genre, Lucy has been putting pen to paper since the first grade, honing her craft and storytelling skills. While Froth, Fiction, and Felony marks her debut in fiction, Lucy is no stranger to the literary world. She is the author of the popular cookbook, Kitchen Meets Girl: 30 Easy Meals for Reluctant Cooks, which has helped countless readers find joy and confidence in the kitchen.

When she's not writing, Lucy enjoys spending time with her husband and son, cuddling with her cat Lightening, watching college football, and following Drum Corps International. A passionate cook and an avid fan of chips and queso, Lucy often finds culinary inspiration for her stories from her kitchen adventures.

Stay Connected with Lucy:

Website: www.lucypenbrook.com
Newsletter: Sign up at her website to get the exclusive prequel novella, *Books, Brew, and Beginnings*, for FREE!
Instagram: @lucypenbrookauthor
Facebook: Lucy Penbrook – Cozy Mystery Author

Join Lucy's community to stay updated on her latest releases, special offers, and behind-the-scene glimpses into her writing journey. Happy Reading!

Coming Soon in the Piper Page Cozy Mystery Series

Cocoa, Carols, and Conspiracy – A Maplebrook Christmas Novella

Just when Piper Page thought she could cozy up with a mug of cocoa and a good book, the town's First Annual Cookie Crawl turns deadly. When the beloved choir director drops dead before the tree lighting, Piper and the Murder Mystery Book Club must sift through powdered sugar, holiday rivalries, and peppermint-flavored secrets to catch a killer before Christmas goes cold.

A festive whodunit filled with cookies, carols, and one very suspicious Santa.

Available October 15, 2025

Visit www.lucypenbrook.com to stay updated!

Recipes from The Sugar Whisk & Books and Brew

Where every cozy mystery pairs best with something sweet... and possibly caffeinated.

In Maplebrook, mystery-solving is best done with a full belly and a well-caffeinated brain. Whether it's a slice of Evie's famous banana bread or one of Piper's iced lattes, these recipes have fueled more than one clue hunt. Now you can bring a little slice of Books and Brew into your own kitchen. Cat sidekick optional—but highly recommended.

Piper's Favorite Banana Bread

As seen in "Froth, Fiction, and Felony"

Evie bakes this warm, comforting banana bread in small batches every morning—just enough to tempt even the most health-conscious Maplebrook locals. Piper swears by it for solving crimes... and breakfast.

Ingredients

- 2 very tired bananas (brown spots = flavor gold!)

- 2 cups (248g) all-purpose flour, spooned and leveled

- ½ teaspoon salt

- 1 teaspoon baking soda

- 1 cup (200g) granulated sugar, plus more for the pan

- ½ cup (113g) unsalted butter, softened (plus more for greasing)

- 2 large eggs

- 7 tablespoons (103ml) milk

- 1 teaspoon vinegar or lemon juice
  (*Or swap both for buttermilk—see notes!*)

Instructions

1. Preheat your oven to 375°F. Grease a 9x5x3" loaf pan with **real butter**, then dust the pan with about 2 tablespoons of sugar. Swirl it around until the sides and bottom are coated in sweet sparkle.

2. In a small bowl, mash the bananas with a fork or potato masher until smooth-ish.

3. In another bowl, whisk together the flour, baking soda, and salt.

4. In a large bowl, cream the butter and sugar until fluffy. Add mashed bananas and eggs, and mix until just combined.

5. Add the dry ingredients, milk, and vinegar. Stir gently until the batter comes together—it'll still be a little lumpy.

6. Pour into the prepared pan and smooth the top. Bake for 50–60 minutes, or until a toothpick comes out with a few moist crumbs.

7. Cool for at least 15–20 minutes before slicing. Or don't. Piper never waits.

Evie's Notes:
- Got buttermilk? Use it and skip the vinegar.

- No vinegar? Lemon juice will do.

- Dairy-free? Any milk will work in a pinch.

Piper's Iced Caramel Latte

As seen in "Froth, Fiction, and Felony"

Whether she's chasing suspects or shelving mysteries, Piper swears by this sweet, chilled pick-me-up. Bonus: it pairs perfectly with banana bread and mild peril.

Caramel Simple Syrup *(makes 6–8 servings)*

- ½ cup granulated or coconut sugar

- ½ cup water

- ½ tsp vanilla extract

- *Optional: pinch of salt for a salted caramel twist*

Instructions:

1. Combine sugar and water in a saucepan over medium-high heat. Stir until sugar dissolves (about 2 minutes).

2. Cover and let boil for 2–3 minutes.

3. Remove lid and stir gently until syrup turns light amber.

4. Remove from heat, stir in vanilla (and salt if using).

5. Let cool and store in the fridge. Piper keeps hers close at hand—right next to her emergency espresso stash.

Iced Caramel Latte (Single Serving)

- 1–3 tbsp caramel syrup (to taste)

- 1 cup milk of choice (whole, oat, almond, etc.)

- 1–2 shots espresso or strong coffee, cooled

- 1 cup ice

- Optional: whipped cream + caramel drizzle

Instructions:

1. Stir caramel syrup into milk and froth lightly if desired.

2. Fill a tall glass with ice.

3. Pour in the caramel milk mixture.

4. Add espresso on top. Stir gently.

5. Top with whipped cream and more caramel if your day needs extra cozy.

Piper's Tip:

Pairs best with a stack of mystery novels, a cat curled up nearby, and zero plans to leave the house.

Want More Recipes, Clues, and Cozy Charm?

If you loved these sweet bites and sips from Maplebrook, you're in for a treat—Evie's whisk is always working, and Piper's espresso machine never sleeps.

More recipes from *The Sugar Whisk* and *Books and Brew* will be featured in upcoming Piper Page Cozy Mysteries!

Bonus recipes, deleted scenes, and sneak peeks are shared exclusively with my email subscribers.

Join the Murder Mystery Book Club (no actual murders required):

Sign up at www.lucypenbrook.com to get delicious updates and your invite to the coziest corner of the mystery world.